*Merry Christmas Mitzi 2007*

*A So Sophisticated Publication*

# When I'm Loving You

*K. Lowery Moore*

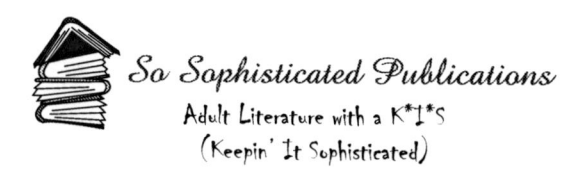

So Sophisticated Publications
Adult Literature with a K*I*S
(Keepin' It Sophisticated)

So Sophisticated Publications
P.O. Box 23002
Washington, DC 20026-3002

WHEN I'M LOVING YOU. Copyright © 2007 by K. Lowery Moore.

All rights reserved, including the right of reproduction in whole or in part in any form. No part of this book may be used or reproduced in any manner, whatsoever, without permission except in the case of brief quotations embodied in critical articles and reviews. For information, address So Sophisticated Publications, P.O. Box 23002, Washington, DC 20026-3002.

All So Sophisticated books may be purchased for education, business, or sales promotional use. For information, please write: Special Markets Department, So Sophisticated Publications, P.O. Box 23002, Washington, DC 20026-3002.

**Author's Note**

Although this is a work of fiction, some of the characters and situations presented in this book were inspired by actual people and events. Most of the situations were embellished for an extra dramatic appeal. All parties presented in the book have been notified, however, the names were changed to protect the innocent, as well as the guilty.

All poems included in this novel are original works by the author and may have been edited from its original creation to fit in within the story.

ISBN-13: 978-0-9795333-1-0
ISBN-10: 0-9795333-1-7

LCCN: 2007906062

Cover & Interior Designed by The Writer's Assistant
www.thewritersassistant.com

Printed in the United States of America

*This book was written in loving memory of my mother*
*Ernestine Lowery Moore*
*(1941-1983)*

## For My Mother

Today and everyday I know you are smiling down on me
And I hope you are proud of the woman I've turned out to be
All that I've done and all that I do
Mama, is in the honor of you

You are the source of my strength to keep me striving for the best
I admired you so, you made motherhood seem effortless
Never complaining, putting your children's needs in front of your own
I just wish you were here to see how we have grown

These past 24 years have been so hard without you here
Especially on Mother's Day, I just wish you could be near
Your picture hangs on my wall to soothe me when I'm sad
Plus your grandsons can see what a beautiful mother I had

But again, I know you're in Heaven smiling down
I would just prefer to have you around
Mama, sometimes I need you especially when the world is not so friendly
But I always live by the values you've instilled in me

To always be strong and walk with my head held high
Carry myself like a lady and never be afraid to cry
To always have dignity and a sense of self respect
Because when all else fails that's all you have left

So, Mama, as you can see, your baby girl is okay
In my heart you will always stay

# Acknowledgments

First and foremost, I have to thank God for my existence. Those who know me may not know that on August 8, 2004, I almost became a memory. I was struck by a stray bullet that missed my spine by less than an inch. Since then, I have been living my life to the fullest and have stopped saying, "I'm going to do this tomorrow" because tomorrow may never get here. That incident gave me the push I needed to pursue my dream of being a published author.

I want to thank my mother and guardian angel, the late Ernestine Lowery Moore, for having me. Mama, I know it was probably a hard decision because you were already trying to survive as a single mother raising three other bad kids (smile). Although you are not physically here, I know you are here watching over me. I hope I make you proud.

To my father, Herman Sr., I know you don't feel appreciated, but, Daddy, I am very grateful for the things you have taught me throughout the years. I was actually listening to you.

To Mary, you are the best stepmother a child could possibly have. You were there for me as if I was truly your own birth daughter and you are still here for me although I am an adult. I can't begin to express the love I have for you.

To my siblings: Judy, Angela, and H. Marcellus Jr. This world would be a lonely place without you. We have all struggled with the loss of our mother but we have managed to become wonderful adults when we could have very well turned out to be drug addicts or something worse. Marcus, though we only share a paternal parent, you are still one of us. You can't escape the Moore curse. Just kidding!

I know we aren't supposed to have favorites in our family. However, to my cousin Courtney, you are more than family to me; you are one of my best friends. Keep being a Diva, you've earned it! Thanks for reading my manuscript, in advance, and giving me honest feedback.

To my nephew, Trovon, who is more like a brother to me; keep striving for greatness. I know you have it in you, because you are related to me (smile). Follow your dreams!

To N. Brackett, I pray for your safe return from Iraq. You mean more to me than you will ever know. I'm still mad that you decided to go into the military in the midst of a war. However, I understand that you were fulfilling a dream of your own. I'm so proud of you!

To my friend and mentor, Yonder, what can I say? How is thank you, thank you, thank you? God brought you into my life at the perfect time. Our God is always on time. Thank you for believing in my ability to get this done. No matter how discouraged I became, you kept me focused, always having something positive to say. Check out this author on www.myspace.com/whatidoistaboo.

I want to give an extra special thank you to my editor and literary advisor, Jessica Tilles. You have been a very critical part of my dream, and I am forever grateful. Please check out this ESSENCE best-selling author at www.jessicatilles.com.

To those who believed in my writing ability, this book is especially for you. There were times when I felt discouraged but you kept me motivated—especially my friends at the National Science Foundation, the U.S. Department of

Transportation and the U.S. Department of Housing and Urban Development. You know how we love our good government jobs!

To my family and friends who didn't hesitate to make a contribution to help launch my career as an author. A million thanks to everyone who committed to purchasing my book in advance.

I would also like to mention those authors who have greatly influenced my work: Terry McMillan, the late BeBe Moore Campbell, Mary B. Morrison, and Michael Baisden.

Last, but of course not least, my sons Antonio and Andray. I love you guys more than anything else! Discover your purpose and expand on your abilities. Life is full of endless possibilities.

*My world was once so limited
Now my horizon has been expanded
I have experienced so much
In all the places I have landed*

*Once moving slowly through life
Unsure where the road would lead me
Now I can travel to some of the highest places
I thought I would never see*

*I used to be afraid to venture out
Thinking I could be crushed along with my dream
Now that I've shed my old skin
I've developed into the most beautiful thing*

*My life is that of a Butterfly*

# DEDICATION

This book is dedicated to all the strong, black women who have survived and prospered even in the midst of all kinds of adversity. A special dedication goes out to all the caring, black men that hung in there when we strong, black women seemed emotionally unavailable. This book could not have been written without the positive black male presence I have in my life. Remember sistas and brothas, we are in this together. Black love is alive and well; all we have to do is just pay attention.

# When I'm Loving You

## CHAPTER 1
# NATASHA

**I FELT THE STREAM OF TEARS** fall down my cheeks as I taped the last box of things I packed so far. It has been six months since I buried my only child and the pain is too much to bear. Every room in my four-bedroom townhouse reminds me of my sixteen-year-old daughter whom I will never see alive again. Therefore, I know that it is best for me to move. It was a hard decision, but I decided to sale my house and move into a small two-bedroom condominium that is for rent in a nearby neighborhood. From there I plan to figure out exactly what my next move is going to be. I worked so hard to get this house and to maintain it, that it is actually heartbreaking to move. In the beginning, I struggled to make ends meet, but I tried not to complain.

When my daughter, Aisha, was two years old, her dad decided that he was not ready for a family. He preferred to run the streets, get drunk and smoke weed with his boys. I guess a part of Tyrone hadn't grown up, but I didn't have much of a choice when Aisha was born. I was determined to remain strong and not let his running the streets affect Aisha. She was my priority and I was going to make sure that she had the best of everything. When I suspected Tyrone was selling marijuana, I decided that I should prepare to move out on my own. I was only nineteen years old so I wasn't sure how I was going to make it, but I knew I would have to figure it out along the way.

 I contemplated taking advantage of public assistance, but that wasn't really me to accept handouts. Being in a foster home is one thing; I didn't have a choice where I ended up in the system after my parents died. I was now an adult so I did have a choice. Tyrone's mother, whom I called Ma Price, helped me apply for a federal government job where she worked at the Department of Education. I really wanted to work in a clothing store, but it didn't pay enough money for me to pay bills and take care of Aisha. I was extremely excited when I was hired for the Administrative Assistant job I applied for. Soon after I started working, I moved into a spacious one-bedroom apartment close to Ma Price's house. The apartment had plenty of room for my baby girl and me.

 Tyrone and I weren't together anymore, but his mother was still there for me like when I lived with them. Tyrone resented my relationship with his mother because he thought that was my way of making sure I kept up with what he was doing. In a way, he was right, but I loved his mother. Ma Price was a mother to me as well. She took me in after I told her one of my foster brothers, Bobby, wanted me to have sex with him. He kept saying it was

*When I'm Loving You*

okay since we weren't related by blood, but I still considered him my brother. Since I was almost eighteen when I found out I was pregnant with Tyrone's baby, it was arranged for me to live with Tyrone and his mother. My foster mother said I could continue to stay with her, but I couldn't do that after Bobby kept trying to touch me even after he knew I was pregnant. I was afraid he would try to force himself on me one day. I didn't tell my foster mother what was going on with Bobby because I didn't want to cause any problems for her. I knew she needed the money she was getting for him and the other kids. I didn't want to risk them being taken away from her.

Ma Price died from complications after having stroke a year after I moved out, and Tyrone's smoking and drinking became worse. I know he was hurting from the loss of his mother, but he started living a very destructive lifestyle. He would wake up and smoke a blunt before he would brush his teeth. When he would come to visit Aisha, I could tell he was normally high. I couldn't continue to watch him destroy his life. Therefore, I decided to move from Riverdale, Georgia to Suitland, Maryland since I had friends who lived close to that area and it was affordable. I felt it was necessary for me to leave Georgia in order to avoid running into Tyrone. I needed to move on with my life; I was deeply in love with him and it pained me to see what he was becoming. I had to get over him somehow and focus on being a mother to my daughter.

My job was able to transfer me to the Department of Education headquarters building in Washington, DC. After I settled into my new apartment in Suitland, Maryland, I enrolled in the Bachelor's Degree program for Education at the University of Maryland, University College Campus. Tyrone promised he

**19**

would support Aisha, but my pride would not allow it. I was so stubborn and determined to make it on my own; I didn't want his help. He would try to give me money but I would never accept it. One day he mailed me a check for five hundred dollars and I mailed it back, shredded! I thought it might have been "fast" money from selling drugs and I didn't want it.

Tyrone claimed that he was not ready to commit to a relationship around the time I left Georgia, but that soon changed. He married another woman when Aisha was five years old. That was only two years after I left, and I was crushed. I would try to visit Georgia at least two or three times a year so Tyrone could see Aisha. After his marriage, I stopped going to Georgia. Needless to say, it was the last time Tyrone saw her, except in pictures, until the day of her funeral.

After I learned of Tyrone's marriage, I felt a sense of rejection. I wondered if I wasn't good enough for him to commit to me. Was there something wrong with me? Eventually, I convinced myself that I was too good for him, so those insecure thoughts faded. I kept telling myself things don't work out the way we plan them sometimes. Plus, I realized that we were too young for marriage at the time Aisha was born.

Although Aisha grew up without her dad, she became a promising young woman. I was so proud of her. She was quiet and shy, but she had many friends. She made A's and B's all through high school and, in her junior year, she started applying to colleges. She was getting letters from various universities to visit their campus. But from the time she was in junior high school, she had her heart set on going to Princeton University. She often thought Princeton was out of our financial reach, but ever since Aisha was five years old, I had been saving five

*When I'm Loving You*

hundred dollars per month towards her college education. My federal government job paid enough money for me to be able to save two hundred and fifty dollars per payday.

I purchased my first home in the community of Kettering in Upper Marlboro, Maryland when I reached the GS-9 level, therefore, with any promotion I received after that I could save the net difference. After I received my Master's Degree in Education, I managed to work my way up from an Administrative Assistant, GS-9 to a GS-14 position as an Education Specialist, still within the Department of Education. Although I was making close to one hundred thousand dollars a year, I made sure I lived within my means in order to live comfortably and to prepare for my daughter's future. I managed to save roughly seventy-five thousand dollars, with all the interest accrued, to put towards my daughter's education. As expensive as things were now, that would have only covered about two years of college, if that. It didn't matter because I believed the rest of the money was going to come.

Aisha was as beautiful as she was smart. I hated that boys were calling on the telephone for her, but the way things were these days, I was glad she was interested in boys and not girls. I remember the day when Aisha came to me and asked if we could talk about sex. I wanted a hole to open up and swallow me, but on the other hand, I was glad she was comfortable to come to me. The first thing she said was, "Mom, I am not having sex yet, but I am curious about it." I kept looking around for that hole to appear. I knew what she was going through because I was in the eleventh grade also when I became curious about sex. I felt I didn't have anyone to turn to and that's how Aisha got here.

# K. Lowery Moore

When Aisha's high school arranged a tour of colleges for the top students in their junior class, I didn't want to tell her she couldn't go. She would have not forgiven me and I needed Aisha as much as she needed me. Who would have thought that putting my only child on a bus to attend a college tour would be the last time I would see her alive? The thought of her last few moments being in fear, or in pain, deeply saddens me. Apparently, the driver of an eighteen-wheeler fell asleep, crossed the median into oncoming traffic and collided with the tour bus my daughter was on. When I received a telephone call that night, I thought it was Aisha letting me know that she arrived safely at the first college location. I could not have been more wrong because they never made it to the college tour. It was one of the school administrators calling to notify me of the accident. Many of us lost our children on that day. As painful as it is, I have to continue living without my child. But the question is how?

The sound of the doorbell ringing interrupted my thoughts. I knew it was that damn Tyrone. I didn't turn him away this time because I knew he was hurting over the loss of Aisha too. A lot of his hurt was due to his guilt of not being around for Aisha, which I will admit was partially my fault. I agreed to meet with him since he was in town for a business trip. About a year after Tyrone's mother died, he managed to enroll in college at Georgia State and earned his Bachelor of Science Degree in Accounting. His mother left him a substantial amount of money he used for his college tuition. She would be so proud of him today.

"Hello Tyrone," I said, as I opened the door avoiding eye contact.

"I don't plan to stay long but I wanted to see you before I left town," Tyrone uttered as he tried to hold back his tears.

"What is this about Tyrone?" Trying to sound as if I didn't care, but I did care, I couldn't let him know it.

Before today, the last time Tyrone and I spoke was at Aisha's funeral. My foster mother thought it would have been cruel of me not to let him know about the accident. I couldn't understand how he could act as if he cared when he didn't watch her grow up. I know that's probably not a fair thing to say since I was the one who picked up and moved to another state; keeping Aisha from him. I didn't want him in and out of her life, like some kind of revolving door. Kids don't understand why daddy didn't show up and then mommy has to spend the next few hours consoling a crying child trying to explain what happened. I wasn't having it. Call me stubborn; but Aisha was too important to me to see her hurt period!

When Aisha was about twelve years old, she started asking about her dad so I decided to let her call him. I didn't want her hating me for keeping her from him. Tyrone sent her calling cards and they established a long distance bond. She was so happy. She would have me snapping pictures all day so she could send to him. I thought that was too cute of her to want to do that for him. She loved her daddy although he wasn't physically there. I would have done anything to make sure my daughter was happy, even if it meant dealing with that damn Tyrone.

"I know I didn't always do right by you or Aisha, but I hope that one day you will forgive me," Tyrone said, handing me an envelope.

"I told you I don't want anything from you Tyrone," I bitterly snapped with both hands on my curvaceous hips.

"Please, for once stop being so stubborn and take it. You know there was a time when I was in love with you Tash, and I never stopped caring about you although our relationship didn't work. Take this and you will never have to deal with me again; if you don't want to."

A part of me wanted to cry because he was right; there was a time when we were in love. I don't understand what happened to Tyrone back then. I accepted the envelope. He kissed me on the cheek and walked out of my life and maybe for good that time, who knows? Inside the envelope were a letter and a smaller envelope. I put the smaller envelope in the bible on my nightstand and unfolded the letter. The letter read:

*Dear Natasha,*

*I'm writing this letter in hopes to make amends for hurting you for so many years. It was never my intention for things to turn out the way that they did because you were my first love. I guess I was too young to handle the pressures of a relationship and like a coward, I ran away from my responsibilities and started running the streets. I know sorry is not enough for all the pain that I've caused you, but I need to say it anyway. It has taken me six months to face you after Aisha's funeral. I still can't believe that she is gone. I owe you so much but I know money is not enough to repay you for all that you have gone through raising her. I couldn't handle that you didn't need me. You were woman enough to not put up with my bullshit and to raise our child alone. For that, I deeply admire you. The day Aisha called me for the first time, I was so happy that you finally let her contact me. That filled a void in my life. Ever since you left Georgia, I put money aside each month to surprise the both of you when it was time for her to go to college. I knew she always dreamed of going to a prestigious university and I wanted to make her*

dream a reality. I know you would not have accepted it since you sent my checks back to me shredded. Therefore, I put the money in a money market account. Well I guess I say all of this to say, the money is now yours. It's not much but I wanted you to know that I loved our daughter although I didn't always do a very good job of showing it. Because of me, I know it's been hard for you to trust men and to fall in love. But rest assure, we are not all assholes. You deserve the very best in life so let your guard down, please, for Aisha. She would often tell me that she wanted you to get married and be happy. However, she often felt like she was in the way. Love again, life is way too short not to.
    Always,
    Tyrone

    This was the Tyrone I remembered and fell in love with in high school. I cried so hard, the words started to smear off the letter from my tears. I folded the letter up and placed it in the bible along with the smaller envelope. I wouldn't find out until the next day that inside of the envelope was the information for the money market account that Tyrone opened for Aisha. The paperwork named me as the sole beneficiary. He actually loved his daughter more than I realized.

    Tyrone wrote his cell phone number and the telephone number to his hotel room on the outside of the smaller envelope in case I wanted to talk. I wanted to see him one last time if he was going to walk out of my life forever. When I called, he sounded very happy to hear from me. I asked him if it was okay for me to stop by his hotel room so we could talk, there were so many things I needed to get off my chest to him. He agreed that I could come by later on that evening and he gave me the address to the hotel and his room number.

~ ~ ~ ~ ~

It was a beautiful Friday night and the drive to the hotel was very soothing. I was playing the CD by Kindred. I sang along with my favorite song on the CD, "Far away from here, far away from here. I want to jump in a taxi cab, pack a bag, and getaway fast." That was exactly how I felt; I wanted to get far away from here. After parking my car, I called Tyrone to let him know that I was downstairs in the lobby and I would be up soon. I found Tyrone's hotel room and knocked on the door. I wasn't prepared at all for what was about to take place. When Tyrone opened the door to his hotel room, he was wearing a pair of basketball shorts and a t-shirt with the sleeves cut off. Damn, he looked good. He must have taken a shower before I arrived because he smelled fresh like Dove soap and cologne I couldn't make out.

"What kind of cologne are you wearing?"

"Armani."

"It smells good on you."

"Thank you." Tyrone had a smirk, as if he was surprised at my compliment. "Would you like a glass of wine?"

"Sure, thanks."

He poured me a glass of wine and we toasted to the good ole days. We talked for what seemed like hours but only an hour actually went past. I wanted to make sure he knew there weren't any hard feelings on my end and that I wanted to apologize for moving so far away and keeping Aisha from him. He assured me he never stopped thinking about us and asked me if I had opened

## When I'm Loving You

the other envelope that he had given me. I told him that I would open it when I get home.

As I stood to walk towards the door, Tyrone stepped up close behind me and put his arms around my waist as if to say, "Don't go." *What in the world*, I thought, but I couldn't move or say anything. Part of it was because of the four glasses of wine I had consumed and the other part was because I was, actually, where I wanted to be for that moment. Tyrone started kissing the back of my neck and gently rubbing his fully erect penis on my ass. Again, I couldn't move or say anything. Like a schoolgirl, I stood there and smiled. He turned me around and we started to kiss. *Damn*, I thought to myself as I felt myself becoming instantly moist. After all these years, he still turns me on. I wanted him to stop kissing me, touching me, and grinding on me but my body didn't want him to. Next thing I knew, my shirt was up over my head and my skirt was around my feet, oops! I felt like the R&B singer Tweet in her song *Oops*. Except unlike Tweet, I wasn't alone. I was in Tyrone's arms. Why did I wear this skirt in the first damn place? Too easy! Tyrone looked me straight in my eyes as if to ask for approval to continue. I blinked seductively as if to say, "Take me I'm yours."

After I helped him out of his clothes, he picked me up and carried me over to the king-sized bed. He unhooked my bra with one hand and he then proceeded to pull down my thongs with his teeth. He kissed and caressed my entire body until I couldn't take it any more. My body hadn't had this much attention in a long time so I wasn't about to stop him. I handed him the condom that he took out of his overnight bag. I don't remember him putting it on the pillow although I saw him take it out of the bag. I stroked his penis a few times to make sure he was nice and hard and then he slid on the condom. I was so ready for him that as soon as he climbed on top of me, I grabbed his erection and pushed him inside of me. Ummmmm, I couldn't believe how good it felt. One passionate thrust after another from Tyrone made my eyes roll up in my head. We were sixteen again, but with eighteen more years of experience. After having a series of orgasms, I slept like a baby. I know Tyrone was satisfied because he was snoring before I actually drifted off.

The next morning, I awoke before Tyrone. I decided to get up, wash my face and brush my teeth in case he wanted some morning "nookie." As I walked past the dresser that stood next to the bed, I noticed some paperwork, which looked like court documents, on top of a brown 9 x 12 envelope. I tried not to look at the paperwork, but I swear I couldn't help it. As I looked closer, it was a copy of signed divorce papers. "Damn, he's no longer married," I said quietly to myself as the thrill of sleeping with a married man quickly faded. I decided to act as if I didn't see the divorce papers and proceeded to the bathroom. I guess I was making too much noise because Tyrone almost immediately joined me in the bathroom. He also washed his face and brushed his teeth. *Thank you*, I thought to myself because I hate when a man tries to talk to me in the morning prior to brushing his teeth. He must have remembered me fussing about that when we were together years ago. When we were both done in the bathroom, we climbed back in the bed. I was hungry so I was glad when Tyrone asked if I wanted him to ordered room service. After our order was placed, we kissed and cuddled. Our breakfast arrived about twenty minutes later. While we were eating breakfast, I remembered that Tyrone had a plane to catch back to Georgia.

*When I'm Loving You*

"What time is your flight?" I asked knowing I didn't want him to go.

"I cancelled it for right now."

I asked him why he cancelled his flight and he told me it was because he wanted to spend the weekend with me. *Lord, what have I done*? I said the silent prayer in my head for Tyrone not to hurt me again. I have always known that he was my soul mate and that's why it's been so hard for me to take other men seriously. A part of me has always wanted us to get back together, but he was so irresponsible back then. I don't know if I can trust him. A lot has changed in both of us but I actually think it was for the better. Then my thoughts were interrupted with the reality that I still needed to pack Aisha's room.

"I have to pack Aisha's things this weekend as hard as it's going to be for me." I could feel my eyes start to water.

"I will help you. You shouldn't have to do this alone. You have been so strong through all of this and I want to be there for you." He sounded very sincere as he hugged me.

"Sure, why not. I'm sure Aisha would be glad to see us finally getting along."

"Yeah, I'm sure she's watching over us."

"I hope she wasn't watching us last night," I jokingly said, trying to make light of the situation. Tyrone laughed and nodded.

Dianne and Lynda are going to have a field day with this when I tell them. I can't wait to tell them Sunday at brunch. They are not going to believe that I had sex with Tyrone and great sex at that. Well Dianne may believe it; she had pretty much already predicted it would happen. She gets on my nerves, damn know-it-all, but I love her dearly. I know I will have to hear a lecture from her ass as if she has never done crazy things. I hate that she has that Ph.D. in Psychology. Wasn't it bad enough that she would analyze everything when we were teenagers? *Now Natasha*, I can hear her now.

## Chapter 2

# Dianne

**I WOKE UP AT SIX O'CLOCK AM** from another great night of sleep. *Damn I love this Sleep Number bed*, I thought to myself as I tried to ease out of bed, as not to wake my sound asleep husband. Who would have thought that I, of all women, would find that "right" man to marry? There was always something wrong with most of the men I dated. Either they were too short, too thick, too broke, not educated enough or couldn't fuck and sometimes all of the above.

I had one foot on the floor when Nelson gently grabbed my hand. I knew exactly what that meant. I eased back onto the bed and climbed on top of my man. My God, how I love this man. He is everything I desire in a man, imagine that. He is attractive, educated, successful in his career, attentive and fun to be around. Kind of like the male version of me. I am so in love with him that I often can't get anything done during the day because he clouds my thoughts. After three years of marriage, I was certain the "newness" would wear off. However, it is the opposite. Our marriage becomes more exciting everyday. We do some wild and crazy things together and then we laugh about it for days. That is definitely one of the things I love most about Nelson; he makes me laugh.

When I straddled Nelson, he was fully aroused. I reached over on the nightstand, took out two Listerine strips from the pack, gave one to him and put the other one on my tongue. It was a temporary solution to morning breath. We began to kiss and slowly grind. The head of his dick rubbing against my clit was enough to make me have an orgasm, but I preferred him to be inside of me when that happens. It's nothing like being stroked to an orgasm. I lifted my body enough so I could slide him into my wetness and when I did, Nelson opened his eyes. He grabbed the back of my head and whispered, "Good morning baby," I responded with a "good morning sweetheart." Since we stopped using condoms, the first round of sex doesn't last long. I have my man *cumming* like you wouldn't believe. He is not cool with how fast he ejaculates, but to a woman with an ego like mine, pleasing my man is a very big deal. Therefore, we are content knowing that the first round would belong to him and the second is all about me. I love the fact that it doesn't take Nelson long to get a second erection.

As I slowly went up and down on my husband's power tool, as he like to call it, he grabbed my round ass with both hands and asked me in a pimp daddy voice, "Whose pussy is it?"

Thinking quickly, I sarcastically replied as I ran my long manicured nails down his hairy chest, "It's my pussy but you are welcome to it anytime you like, for a small fee."

*When I'm Loving You*

He laughed and rolled me over so he could be in charge for a while. As controlling as I am, I love him to be in control of sex and everything else. I pretty much let him handle whatever he wanted and my girlfriends couldn't believe it. I was used to running all the men in my life, but Nelson is serious husband material, a keeper for life. As strong and independent as I am, I want him to be the kind of head of the household that grandma used to lecture me about. "You have to allow a man to lead," grandma would always tell my sisters and me. My brother would be like, "yeah" and we would chase him around grandma's backyard until our legs were tired of running. Nelson is the first man I have trusted to lead me anywhere. The rest of them fools would have led me right into the poor house and I simply wasn't having that.

Both of us are making six figures so money is never an issue for us. The lack of money is one of the number one causes of divorce so I'm not worried about that. I'm not even worried about him cheating on me. I'm not saying he never has or he wouldn't cheat, but to be honest, I think he is too worried about me cheating on him. One day he asked me, "What would you do if you found out that I cheated on you?" We were discussing one of his boys who had been caught cheating and his wife burned all of his worldly possessions and even tried to set him on fire while he was sleep. Good thing he woke up when he smelled the gas, but his house burned to the ground along with his new Lexus in the garage. I simply told him that every time he has the urge to fuck another woman, to imagine one of his boys all up in me. He was not happy I said that but I think it worked, who knows? I try not to focus on stuff like that. I plan to have fun and be happy with my husband for however long our marriage last. I hope forever, but I will leave it in God's hands because He knows what's best for us.

One orgasm and two ejaculations later, we headed for the shower. We needed to act as if we both had jobs to go to, especially me because it is my first day on a new assignment. Nelson showered in the master bathroom, as I grabbed my washcloth and towel and headed for the shower in the guest room.

"Dianne, where are you going?"

"I'm going to take a shower in the guest room's bathroom," I answered as I headed out of the French doors of our bedroom.

"Why? Come in here with me."

"Oh no, Nelly!" I said, trying to be funny. I know he hates when I call him that because he knows the famous rapper Nelly is one of my favorite rappers although I wasn't really into rap music anymore. "I have a job to get to and so do you."

"Please!"

"If I come in there, you know what's going to happen; round three and neither one of us can be late today. You have that Senior Executives Meeting at 10:00 a.m. and I have to get to work at least thirty minutes early in order to print out the handouts for my seminar."

"Why didn't you get your assistant to do it?"

"She has better things to do."

"Huh? You are the only person I know with an assistant who doesn't utilize the assistance. Why hire someone if you are going to answer your own phones, schedule your own meetings and seminars, and copy your own handouts?"

"Would you feel better if I call Pamela and ask her to do it so I can come in there with you?"

"Yes, but I told you I'm not going to try nothing else this morning. I've already busted twice and I don't even think I can get it up again right about now. I'm exhausted. Between last night and this morning, you're killing me."

I can't believe I fell for it. As soon as I stepped into the shower, Nelson had another full erection waiting for me.

"Come to daddy," he said with dick in hand.

*I knew it*, I thought to myself as he kissed my neck. I knew it. But I loved it. Once again, my husband was inside of me making me feel as good as he always makes me feel when we make love—incredible, simply incredible!

It's a good thing I have wash and go hair. The erotic shower scene I had with Nelson, had my hair in serious disarray. It was about 7:30 a.m. and my seminar started at 9:30 a.m. As long as I was out of the door by 8:30 a.m., I would be okay. I allowed my hair to air dry until I dressed in my pinstriped pantsuit that fit my curves like you wouldn't believe. Hey, when you've got it, you've got it. I smiled at myself as I admired my size six shape in the mirror. I brushed my shoulder-length hair that had curled naturally on the ends into a neat ponytail. Nelson was dressed dapper and smelling good as always. I went to kiss him goodbye and he grabbed my ass and whispered in my ear, "All right get out of here before we both are unemployed." I can tell he was getting excited again. I don't know what I'm going to do with him, then again, yes I do.

I was lecturing on the topic of Communication Skills to a group of federal government workers and it made me think of when I worked as a Fed. Two years after Nelson and I were married, I quit my job because I was so burned out. I guess Nelson was tired of me always complaining about something that someone did at work because one day he told me, as bluntly as he could, "You need to quit that damn job if you are so unhappy." I didn't think he was serious until he kept asking me if I had typed my resignation letter yet. Quitting the government after fifteen years was hard to do, but I knew my husband had by back. I had my event planning business on the side, but I was used to a regular nine to five. I planned to get back into the government before I lose my years, but it was nice to take a break and pursue something else for a while. I loved my husband even more for allowing me the opportunity to do something else without a hassle. "What a man, what a man, what a mighty good man!" I started singing the Salt 'n Pepa classic aloud as I parked my car.

As an independent contractor, I am certified to teach on a few topics plaguing the federal government and private industry. This would be my last year to work independently if I was to get back in the government without losing any time vested. Nelson didn't see the point of me going back, but he was very supportive and respected my feelings. Damn, I love that man. I was packing my seminar material when memories of how I met Nelson returned.

I was working at the Office of Personnel Management as a Training Specialist. I would visit different federal government sites and train employees on various topics. This particular day, I was at the Pentagon, training a group of managers on ADR, Alternative Dispute Resolution. During that time, I was studying for my Ph.D. in Psychology. I had also managed to write a book. It started out as a dissertation on relationships, but one of my professors was so impressed with my work that he told me I should expand on the subject and consider getting it published. With the help of my professor, a year later, my work was published. Not too many people outside of my university knew that I had written a book. That's why I was surprised when Nelson had a copy of my book with him at the seminar, for me to autograph.

The seminar had ended and I was gathering my things when he walked up to me.

"Great class!"

"Thank you very much," I replied not looking up right away.

When I did look up, our eyes locked for a minute. Nelson was fine. I'm talking Boris Kodje fine. *Wow*, I thought to myself. *They have men like this outside of Hollywood.* My heart pounded as I tried to think of what to say next. That's when I noticed a copy of my book in his hand.

"I was hoping you would autograph your book for me. I thoroughly enjoyed it," he said, smiling showing off his nice teeth and dimples.

"Well thank you. How did you hear about it?"

"A buddy of mine went to your university for grad school and he mentioned it was worth reading. Plus he thought it would be a good idea for us to support a local sista doing her thing. When I found out that you were lecturing today, I figured I would bring my copy with me today to see if you would sign it for me."

"I appreciate that. It didn't make me much money but I did gain some exposure since I wanted to be a motivational speaker. I am actually working on a novel now, but with this job and an event planning business, I'm so tired in the evening that I don't have much time to work on it as I would like to."

"I definitely understand that. Can I walk you to your car?"

"Um, I would say yes, but I caught the metro here today. I parked my car at Branch Avenue Metro Station. Who am I addressing this autograph to?" I asked flirting with my eyes.

"I'm Nelson. Nelson Thompson."

"Well, Nelson it's nice to meet you," I smiled noticing that I didn't see a wedding band. I autographed my book for him and he walked me to the security guard's desk so I could turn in my temporary badge.

"I'm sorry to be so forward, but would you like to meet later this evening for drinks, coffee, or dinner?" Our eyes locked again.

"Sure, that would be very nice. Where do you want to meet and what time?" I responded not trying to sound too excited. I couldn't help it because I hadn't had a stiff one in these sugar walls since that fine ass student intern, Ryan, had bent me over the conference room table about two months prior. He was ten years my junior but there wasn't nothing junior about his dick. *Damn!*

"Call me on my cell phone in an hour and we can go from there. Is that okay?" Nelson said, interrupting my thoughts. He wrote down his number and handed me the paper. Again, our eyes locked.

"That sounds perfect," I said, as I handed him my card.

When his hand touched mine, I felt moisture between my legs. The chemistry between us was unbelievable. As I walked away, I heard the security guard say something to Nelson. He responded but I couldn't hear what he said either. I guess it was some male bonding going on there.

By the time I returned to the office, it was time for me to sign out and go home. I was so excited about my date. *This is a date right?* I thought to myself as I walked out of my office. It had been so long since I went out on a date. I was tired of meeting men not on my intellectual level or lacking the attraction I felt needed to pursue a romantic relationship. Something about him felt different. Damn, I wasn't ready to let my guard down but it was only dinner. I kept thinking to myself, *Dianne, don't get too excited. It's only dinner.* But for some reason it felt like so much more. It was more like love at first sight, if there is really such a thing. Whatever it was, it felt great.

Just then, my cell phone rang and interrupted my thoughts snapping me back to the present day. It was Nelson. "Hi baby, do you want me to pick up something for dinner?" I asked, as I answered my phone.

"Naw, I have it covered. But can you come straight home so we can pick up where we left off this morning?"

I laughed and said, "Sure baby, play with it until I get home. That way it will be nice and hard for me when I walk in the door."

"I'm stroking it now."

"Stop before you make me crash my car," I said, laughing and getting horny.

"Alright, I'll see you in a few. I love you."

"Not as much as I love you." I never thought I would be this much in love with one man. My reminiscing continued.

My first date with Nelson went very well. When he picked me up, he smelled good and looked even better. He asked me if

I had a restaurant in mind, and I told him to decide on the place. I was concerned at first because I wasn't in the mood for one of those upscale, "shi shi" places because I was famished. I'm surprised that he didn't hear my stomach growling, or maybe he did and didn't say anything. I was glad when he said, "Let's go to Outback Steakhouse. I'm in the mood for some real food tonight."

"I'm down," I said, as I grabbed my Kenneth Cole purse and hung it over my shoulder.

During dinner, we barely touched our food. Between our conversations were silent stares into each other's eyes. The waitress brought us boxes so we could take our food home and we left the restaurant. We arrived at my house and Nelson walked to me the door. He was a perfect gentleman all evening.

"I had a really nice time Nelson."

"I did too," he said, as he pulled me close and kissed me.

I am not a big kisser but I wasn't about to stop him. We kissed for five minutes and that's a long time for a kiss. Our first kiss was so special. I was wondering if he was feeling the same thing that I was feeling, strong chemistry. We would kiss for a few minutes, pull away and look at each other, and then kiss again. Finally, I asked if he wanted to come in for a few minutes. I was glad that he agreed because my nosey neighbor across the street was looking at us out of the window.

I'm glad I keep my place neat. I can't leave my house with things out of place. Nelson sat down on the sofa and I asked him if he wanted a glass of wine.

"Sure beautiful," he answered licking his lips.

I poured two glasses of White Zinfandel and walked over to the sofa, sat down beside him, and handed him one of the glasses.

I picked up the remote to the stereo and turned it on. I keep several of my favorite CD's in rotation. As he looked around the living room, he noticed a Scrabble game on the bottom of the bookshelf. I thought to myself, *no this dude doesn't want to play a game,* because I had other things in mind.

"Ooh, let's play Scrabble," he said, sounding like a little boy.

"You like Scrabble, huh?" I asked sounding competitive knowing I did not want to play Scrabble at that time.

"I'm the champion at this game."

"We'll see about that." I pulled the game off the bookshelf.

About halfway through the game, I thought it would be interesting for me to start spelling suggestive words. My first suggestive word was *vagina.* He looked up at me and nodded as if to say, "It's on." Nelson's next word was *lick* and I followed with *orgasm,* and you know it was a triple word score. Needless to say, we didn't finish that game. We started kissing as if we were high school sweethearts. As he caressed my breasts, I let out a deep sigh. Noticing that was a very sensitive area, he pulled up my shirt and bra and starting sucking on my breasts. He licked, sucked and teased each nipple to make sure both of them received the same amount of attention. In between sucking my breasts, he would look up at me and kiss me on the lips.

I was so turned on by his caressing that I decided to get up and do a little striptease for him. It was so exciting because he played right along as he reached in his pocket to see how much money he had. He licked his finger and counted out his money and then he motioned for me to come closer. The perfect song had made its way through the rotation—*Say Yes* by the duo Floetry. As I danced and unbuttoned my shirt, I mouthed the words to the song as Floetry sang, "All you gotta do is say yes." He nodded his head and rubbed his penis to let me know that he was very much turned on.

When I was down to my Frederick's of Hollywood black and hot pink lace bra and thong set, Nelson placed a twenty-dollar bill under the skinny side strap of my thongs. I giggled like a schoolgirl as I straddled him. While I took off his shirt, he caressed my ass. I unbuttoned and unzipped his pants, then I slowly pulled them down. His boxers soon followed. I was anxious to reveal what he was rubbing while I did my strip tease. While I stroked his dick, he moaned. I then stopped and thought to myself, *what am I doing? How much did I have to drink?*

"What's wrong?" he asked noticing my hesitation.

"I don't know if we should be doing this."

"Why?" Nelson asked obviously disappointed.

"Because we met today, and—"

"And what? You like me right?" Nelson said, interrupting me.

"I really don't know you."

"Well let me rephrase that. You are attracted to me right?"

"Yes, but—"

Nelson kissed me before I could finish my statement. He pulled out a condom from his pocket and asked me, "Are we going to use this or should I put it back in my pocket?"

I wish he didn't smile at me because those dimples are too cute. I stood up and slowly pulled down my thongs. Nelson opened the condom pack and slid on the protection.

I straddled him again, but this time he was inside of me. As I moved up and down, he moaned and said, "Girl, you are so wet. Why didn't you want me to have this? Aw, man, your pussy feels good."

"And you feel so good inside of me," I said, before I started kissing his neck.

Right there on my sofa we became more acquainted—good conversation, good food, and great sex. What more could I ask for in one night?"

When I felt my body about to explode, I whispered in his ear. "I'm about to cum, fuck me harder." That must have turned him on even more because he gave my ass a gentle smack and began to thrust harder up in me. As my juices flowed, I could feel his manhood throbbing inside of me. *He must be cumming too*, I thought.

"Damn, that was good," he said, sounding out of breath.

"Yes it was."

Although the sex was beyond incredible, I was so mad at myself for doing this again. I was so tired of meaningless sex. I got up and went upstairs to my bathroom to wash up. I stared at myself in the mirror and thought to myself, *another one-night stand*. After I washed up, I went back downstairs expecting him to be dressed and ready to leave. I was wrong. He was sitting there with his head in his hand as if he was mad at himself too.

"Would you like to come upstairs and wash up before you go?"

"Are you putting me out already?" Nelson asked seemingly perplexed.

"No, I thought—"

"You thought I was like those other dudes who want to fuck you and go home smiling. That's not me, well not anymore. I'm so tired of meaningless sex but the moment felt so right between us."

"So, sexing me was meaningless?" I asked trying to hold back my emotions.

"Dianne, look. I'm getting too old for wham, bam, thank you ma'am. I feel so close to you that it's tripping me out. I can't explain my feelings to you, but all I know is I'm not ready to go home yet. So do you mind if we lie together and watch a movie or something?"

"No, I don't mind at all."

"And if I get my food out of my car, would you mind heating it up for me? I'm famished. You wore me out girl."

"I was thinking the same thing," I said to him laughing.

૱ ૱ ૱ ૱ ૱

Love at first sight is definitely real in my opinion. I was in love with Nelson from the moment I saw him. We continued to date consistently for the next several months and everything was great. That is until the day he came over to my house and told me something that I didn't want to hear. He told me that he was considering another position in Boston and if he accepted the job, he had three months before it was time for him to move. He saw the sadness in my eyes. He looked at me and wiped away my tears.

"Dianne, this is the job I've been waiting for."

"That's odd because a few months ago, I was the woman you've been waiting for." I turned my back on him and asked him to leave. For the next two weeks, I wouldn't accept any of his calls. I was hurting so badly and I was tired of crying myself to sleep at night.

I didn't hear from Nelson for about a month before the day he showed up at my house. I was so angry with him. He knew how I felt about people showing up unannounced.

"Please don't be mad Dianne, but I had to see you and you weren't answering any of my calls."

"Why do you need to see me? Your dream job is waiting for you in Boston."

"Don't do this, I love you."

"Love me? Is this how you show love? You get another job and leave."

"Can we talk inside, please?" Nelson started to notice the audience of my neighbors. They were probably waiting for him to hit me so they could call the police.

"What do you want, a good-bye fuck?" I started crying hysterically.

I can tell he wasn't prepared for my scene because he grabbed me in his arms and walked me to my door.

"Dianne baby, please stop crying. I'm sorry. I won't go."

"You're only saying that to shut me up."

"No, no. I don't want to lose you. Jobs come and go but finding your soul mate may only come once in a lifetime and I won't go if you don't come with me."

"What?"

"Yeah, that's what I came to talk to you about." He pulled a small box from his pocket and knelt down on one knee.

"Stop. Get up, please." I was starting to get embarrassed because now my neighbors were really looking at us.

"I've been thinking about this for the past month," he started saying while still down on one knee. "I tried to forget about you. I tried to convince myself that you are just another woman that has come into my life for a short time, but that's not true. I am in love with you, Dianne Marshall, and I want you to be my wife whether we live here in Maryland or Massachusetts."

I was so overjoyed. "I don't know what to say."

"Say yes baby, and then help your man up off the ground. I'm not as young as I used to be."

*My man, is that what he said?* I thought to myself. I put my hands on my hips and said, "My man, how do you know I'm going to say yes?"

"Because Dianne, I know you love me. You wouldn't have caused a scene outside of your house if you didn't love me. Now for real, help me up because I told you that I hurt my knee a year ago."

I helped him up, looked him in the eyes and said, "Yes, I'll marry you. Now put my ring on my finger so I can go and call my girls."

He laughed and said, "That's my baby."

A few of my nosey neighbors had the nerve to start clapping. We went inside and made love for hours. We had a month worth of love making to make up.

I love reminiscing about how I met Nelson. Who would have thought that a one-night stand would develop into a marriage? We were married almost one year after we met, and I had the wedding of my dreams.

I pulled up to our house in Fort Washington, MD at about 6:30 p.m. It was such a beautiful Friday evening, so I sat in my car for a few more minutes, smiling at the thoughts of how

I met Nelson. Before I got out of my car, my cell phone rang again. This time it was Lynda debating if she was going on a date with her friend Marlon, whom she didn't plan to take out of the "friend zone." After I hung up the phone, I grabbed my purse, got out of my car and hit the alarm. When I walked inside of our house, all of the lights were either turned off or dimmed very low.

"Nelly baby, where are you?"

"I'm upstairs in the bedroom baby."

The aroma inside was a mixture of roast beef, scented candles, and who knows whatever else.

"Oh, I see you cooked dinner tonight," I yelled before I made it to the top of the stairs.

"Come and see what else your husband has for you."

When I reached our bedroom, I opened the French doors and noticed the trail of red rose petals leading to the bathroom. The lights were out but I allowed the flickering of the candlelight to guide my way to the bathroom. Soft music was playing in the background. Before I entered the bathroom, Nelson walked out, kissed me, and gently caressed my ass. He took me by the hand and led me into the bathroom. Candles were everywhere around the bathroom. The Jacuzzi tub was full of bubbles.

"What's the occasion?"

"You're my wife and I love you."

"What did you do, Nelson Thompson?" I asked with my hands on my hips.

"Nothing baby, I said you're my wife and I love you. I don't need a reason to celebrate our marriage, do I?'"

"No, but—"

## K. Lowery Moore

"There you go trying to analyze everything. Rest that psych degree for a moment and enjoy your bath."

Nelson undressed me and then led me to the tub. He insisted on washing me up. Reluctantly, when I pulled myself out of the relaxing bath, I noticed a Victoria Secret's box on the bed. I smiled to myself. Is it possible to love him any more than I already do? He noticed me admiring the contents of the box. "Put that on and I'll be right back."

I put on the long black lace nightgown that was in the box. It was completely see-through with a long split on both sides. The dip was so low in the back that it stopped right above my firm, round ass. When Nelson came back into the room, he was carrying a bowl of fruit.

"Damn, I knew that would look amazing on you," Nelson said, looking at me as if he was seeing me for the first time.

Nelson fed me grapes and strawberries, one by one, while I lay on the bed like Queen Nefertiti. I was so horny. But every time I tried to initiate intercourse, he would look at me and say, "Hold on, we'll get to that soon enough." After the fruit appetizers, he carried me downstairs to a candlelight dinner. How is this for treatment? In front of my plate was a handwritten note that read:

*Dianne,*
*When a man finds a woman like you, he has to appreciate her everyday in every way possible, not only on special occasions. So today, I want to celebrate our marriage for no reason in particular other than I love you!*
*Love,*
*Your Nelly*

*When I'm Loving You*

The dinner Nelson prepared was very good, but the sex we had afterwards was incredible. Nelson was obviously feeling experimental because he was doing things he hadn't done before. I told him before we were married that I was willing to try almost anything at least once. I guess this was the night he was going to put me to the test.

Nelson had the bottle of flavored lubricant I had purchased at one of the many pleasure parties I attended, not that I needed a lubricant for this wet pussy, but I love bringing home new things for us to try. I initially purchased the flavored lubricant to give Nelson's power tool some flavor since I started "swallowing." The first time I decided to do that, I think Nelson fell in love with me all over again. Normally he announces to me when he is about to cum so I can take his penis out of my mouth and stroke him to an orgasm with my hand. Well this particular time when he said he was about to cum, I kept my mouth wrapped his love stick and swallowed all of my husband's liquids. Nelson made sounds that I had never heard him make before. Afterwards, he stared into my eyes as if he was seeing me for the first time. I guess going to that Taboo Talk Tour paid off. But what is it about a woman swallowing that really excites a man? I guess some things aren't meant for us to understand.

Anyway, Nelson took the lubricant and squeezed it all over my vagina. He licked my clit as he slid his finger in and out of my pussy. It felt so good; I didn't want him to stop. Then he squeezed the lubricant all over my asshole. I thought to myself, *Oh shit I'm about to get my salad tossed.* He licked my rectum as if it was his last meal. Damn, I surprisingly enjoyed every minute of it.

When he was done licking and sucking, it was time for penetration. The head of his dick kept bypassing my vaginal opening sliding towards my ass. *He must be lost*, I thought to myself before he slid the head into my ass. I immediately tensed up but Nelson kept pleading with me to relax. He promised to be gentle as he went in further and further. It wouldn't have been so bad if he was working with something smaller like six or seven inches, with a slim width, but that was not the case. Nelson's nine inches and thick width was about to make me holler but not in a good way. I could tell he was enjoying it so I managed to relax, allowing my husband this hopefully one time anal experience with his wife. This was the only time I was happy to see him cum quickly.

I'll tell you everyday of our marriage is a new and exciting sexual adventure. I guess that's what happens when you find someone who is compatible with you. There is never a dull moment. Now we have our share of disagreements but it's normally regarding where we are vacationing this year or who *came* first yesterday. I don't understand why my friend Lynda is so against marriage. She always tells me what Nelson and I have is a rare find and that most people are not that fortunate to marry their soul mate.

## Chapter 3

# Lynda

"I REALLY DON'T WANT TO GO on this date," I said to Dianne before I hung up the phone. As I admired myself in the mirror, I could see the guilt in my eyes for misleading Marlon like this. He is such a nice guy; a nice guy who I'm not attracted to. We have fun together and great conversation but that isn't enough. Why? Why can't I find a nice guy that I also have chemistry with? I actually have a few times when I was younger, but I always blew it with my attitude. Now that I've grown up, where are they?

I'm not against marriage as Dianne thinks I am, but I doubt if I will ever get married. I've always regretted letting Justin get away. I was so stubborn, refusing to tell him how I really felt about him. When I did, it was too late; he had already put a ring on someone else's finger. I wasn't sure, at the time, where I stood with having a family and Justin was ready for children.

I guess he couldn't wait for me to make up my mind because last I heard his wife had their first child a year ago and she was pregnant again. I guess he found someone to give him that instant family that he longed for. It hurt for a while, but I made the right decision not to rush into anything until I was sure I was ready. I think it was the right decision anyway.

When Marlon arrived, he came up to the door and rang the doorbell. He didn't call from his cell phone as most guys do these days. He brought me a beautiful flower arrangement. He is always so thoughtful. I didn't want to continue to lead him on anymore so I figured that tonight I would tell him the truth about how I felt. I wasn't sure how I was going to go about doing that without hurting his feelings.

During dinner, I looked down at my plate of half-eaten food. Marlon could tell that something was on my mind.

"What's on your mind, beautiful?"

As I looked into his eyes, I knew he could tell that whatever I was about to say wasn't going to be favorable. "Marlon, you are a wonderful man. Any woman would be a fool not to appreciate you. But I don't feel any chemistry between us."

"Oh, well, I understand."

"So, I didn't feel it was right for me to continue to go out with you and mislead you."

"Lynda, I appreciate your honesty. I kind of had a feeling that you weren't really feeling me because there isn't any passion in your kissing or lovemaking."

I was stunned by his response. "It doesn't bother you?"

"Of course it does. Men want to be desired by their women just like women want to be desired by their men, but if it's not there then it's not there."

"I'm really sorry."

"Don't be. It was definitely fun getting to know you and I will always be there for you if you need me."

I felt really terrible. Marlon didn't talk to me the entire ride home. When we pulled up to my house, he got out the car, as usual, and came around to open my door. He walked me to the door and gave me a hug. The look in his eyes was way too painful for me. I really cared about him, but it didn't seem like enough for a romantic relationship. He grabbed my hand and kissed it gently.

"You'll always be special to me, Lynda. I'm sorry that I'm not that one for you," he said to me before he turned and walked away.

I did the right thing, didn't I?

ے ے ے ے ے

As I prepared for bed, I thought about Taye, a guy I met about a year ago. From the moment I saw him, I wanted to get to know him. I am aggressive when it comes to men, but for some reason I was intimidated to approach Taye. Taye works at the fitness center as a personal trainer where I work part-time as a dance instructor. Before I became a dance instructor, I was enrolled in an aerobics class when I first saw him. I wanted to be near him so badly, that I applied for the vacant position as a dance instructor the next day. Going to work on the weekends started to feel like I was going to high school. When I knew I was going to see him, I would make sure I dressed extra cute that day. I didn't even know, at the time, whether or not he was single, or even gay, because you never know these days. However, I knew I was going to find out, somehow.

While in bed, I thought about the night I was out at a nightclub on the Southwest Waterfront, in Washington, DC, with my best friends Dianne and Natasha, when I saw Taye. At that time, I had been working at the fitness center for an entire year, and all he ever managed to say was hello. I gave up on getting to know him on a personal level, but I continued to work at the center anyway, although it was originally my motive to get to know him. I didn't think he had been paying me any attention so I decided to walk past him without speaking. When I walked by, Taye grabbed my hand.

"Hey Lynda, how are you?"

"I'm good. Taye right?" I asked knowing I already knew his name. Taye had the sexiest locks I've ever seen on a man, which complemented his chocolate brown skin. His athletic build didn't make it easy for me to try to ignore him.

"Yes, what brings you out tonight?" he asked still holding on to my hand.

"Girls night out, that's all."

"I can dig it. I hope I'm not holding you up," Taye said, as he noticed Natasha and Dianne standing off to the side with their arms folded.

"Well, not really," I responded as I looked to my friends for their understanding. They smiled acknowledging that they understood that he was someone I really wanted to talk to.

When Taye and I were about to have a conversation at the bar, the DJ started playing reggae music and I loved this genre of music. He noticed me moving my head so he pulled me on the dance floor.

"Let's dance. I see you like reggae too."

## *When I'm Loving You*

I couldn't even respond. I followed him to the dance floor. We danced very seductive with each other and I loved every minute of it. This kind of music requires you to wind your body and I was sure 'nuff winding. I was going to make him remember this night if it was the last thing I did. As I swayed my hips from left to right, Taye was behind me moving right along with me. He was so close to me that I could feel what he was packing in his pants. And man was he packing! The next song was a slow temp reggae jam. I wanted to stop dancing but Taye held me close to him. He turned me around and I put my arms around his neck while his arms were around my waist. Every now and then, he would move his hands down and gently squeeze my ass. A few times, he put his hand inside of my jeans. I couldn't believe I was allowing him to do this, but it felt so good finally being in his arms I wasn't about to stop him. There were a few times that I thought he was actually going to kiss me, but of course, he never did.

When the song was over, I was hoping that Taye would either ask for my number or give me his, but he didn't. He thanked me for the dance and told me that he would see me around the center. I was not happy at all. Natasha and Dianne noticed me pouting.

"Aw girl, come on. You'll see that man soon enough," Natasha said.

"Yeah girl. Come on, but damn he's fine," Dianne had to add.

That night, I left the club feeling horny. I was going to call someone when I got to my car, but who was the lucky man going to be. As I scrolled through the list of numbers in my cell phone, I decided it was going to be Maurice. He was one I could fuck without attachment, mainly because he wasn't trying to commit.

Maurice and I use to date years ago, but he wasn't the most stable man. Every few months he seemed to have a different cell phone number. I was beginning to think he was running from the law. He was also sort of like Natasha's daughter's father, Tyrone. That type of man is more concerned with drinking and getting high. Women didn't really fit into their lives except when it was time to bust a nut. But damn was he fine. Maurice was tall, dark-skinned with a sexy ass beard, the kind that connects with the haircut. I loved this man so much that it almost took therapy to get him out of my system. I never could understand the hold he had on me. I wouldn't see him for months at a time, but I swear every time I would see him it was like meeting him for the first time all over again.

I still couldn't get to sleep, and I was getting horny thinking about that last time I was with Maurice. I was also thinking about Marlon. I hope I didn't hurt his feelings too badly but I felt I should be honest with him. Normally he calls me when he gets home but tonight he didn't. Oh well. I continued thinking about that night. I wondered what Taye was doing or whom he was doing after he left me at the club feeling horny. Who did he think he was seducing me on the dance floor like that and then walking away? When I decided to call Maurice, I was hoping he answered the phone, because at that time, I wasn't ready to pull my Chocolate Dream, a vibrator that I bought from a pleasure party, out of the box yet. When I called, he answered on the first ring.

"Ms. Davis, what's up wit' ya?" Maurice's sexy ass voice said, as he answered his cell phone. Either he must know my number by heart or has me programmed into his cell phone. I'm probably programmed as "Booty Call."

"You," I responded in a serious tone. "I'm horny as hell, what's up?"

"Is this a booty call Ms. Davis?"

"Yes, my booty's calling for you," I said, laughing because I was thinking about R. Kelly's song, "Your Body's Calling."

"Is that right?"

"Stop playing with me and let me come over."

"What do you want to do to me?"

"You'll find out, so have *my* dick ready."

"Damn, it's like that."

"Damn right. This pussy needs you tonight."

"Oh a'ight, be on your way then."

"Okay, see you in a few," I said, already putting my clothes back on. Anytime Maurice answers the phone at 2:00 a.m., he wants it as much as I do.

When I arrived at his apartment, one of his boys was passed out on the floor of his living room either too high or too drunk to go home.

"Don't mind him. He's out," Maurice said, as he walked around his friend in route to his bedroom. I followed behind him because at this point I didn't care who was there; I was ready to get down to business. Inside his room, I pushed him back on the bed after he locked his door. I pulled down his shorts and boxers and pulled out his dick. I stroked his shaft a few times before I circled and teased the head with my tongue.

"Damn girl, that feels good."

"Yeah?"

"Yeah, but come here it's about penetration right now."

"I ain't mad at you," I said, in agreement to his demand.

With each stroke, I was falling for him again. But the crazy thing is I was also thinking about Taye. I wondered what it would be like for him to be inside of me. Taye didn't really seem to be interested though so I'm starting to wonder if he's gay. That must be it. *Yeah he's gay.* I thought as Maurice continued to stroke me to an orgasm.

I woke up that next morning about 7:00 a.m. I kissed Maurice on his forehead and started getting dressed. It was a Saturday morning and I had to get ready for my first dance class. Plus I needed some time to get myself extra cute for Taye. *Hopefully he's working today.* I thought to myself as I stepped over the guy still sleeping on Maurice's living room floor. During the drive to my house, I couldn't help but think about Taye. I would have rather went home with him that night instead of fucking Maurice. I don't know if Maurice even cares about me. *Did he even notice me leaving?* I wondered to myself before my thoughts shifted back to Taye. I was determined to get Taye's attention. I had to think of something alluring. I really hope he isn't gay.

When I arrived at work, after going home for a quick shower, Taye was at the entrance to the gym. "Good morning Taye. How are you this morning?"

"I'm good sexy, how are you?"

*Did he say what I think he said?* I thought to myself as I started to feel moisture between my legs. "I'm feeling well this morning." Partially because I had a powerful orgasm a few hours ago but of course, I kept that to myself.

"Glad to hear that. Do you have a minute to talk?"

"Sure, my first class doesn't start for another twenty-five minutes."

I followed Taye to an office I believed to be the owner of the gym's office. Once inside the office is when I realized that Taye was actually the owner of the gym. I was immediately impressed.

"Lynda, I have been watching you for a while and I was wondering if you were in a situation."

"A situation?" I asked avoiding the question I knew he was asking.

"Yeah, are you seeing anyone special?"

I'm not in a committed relationship if that's what you are asking.

"Well that's good," Taye said, as he walked closer to me.

I immediately became uncomfortable with the situation. He made me nervous for some reason, but in a good way if that makes any sense. Taye grabbed me by my waist and pulled me closer to him. "I have been wondering what it would be like to kiss you."

Before I could even answer him, Taye kissed me inserting his tongue into my mouth. I guess he couldn't have known that I had a dick in my mouth the night before. *Damn his tongue tasted sweet, what did he have for breakfast?* I thought to myself. At first, I tried to pull away from him, but then I realized that I really couldn't fight it any longer. After kissing for a few seconds, I finally was able to pull away.

"Taye, what are you doing?"

"You want me to stop?"

"I don't want this to get out hand, because I have to get ready to teach a class soon."

"I know, we can we pick up with this later?"

"Pick up with what Taye?"

Avoiding my question, he then kissed me again and said, "I also wonder what it would be like to be inside of you."

"Huh, how long have you been wondering that?"

"I don't know but I didn't think it was a good idea at first because you work here. But after dancing with you, I can't fight it any more. I want you."

*Want me!* I couldn't believe it. My hard work of getting Taye to notice me had finally paid off. I couldn't wait to get to know him better. Much better! I continued to date Marlon, until tonight, while Taye and I became more acquainted. Taye sparked a fire inside of me that Marlon never ignited. *I am ready to focus on Taye to see where it can lead*, were my thoughts before I finally fell asleep.

## CHAPTER 4

# PACKING AISHA'S ROOM

**PACKING AISHA'S ROOM** was definitely going to be much harder than I thought. I knew it was going to be difficult but I was not at all prepared for the emotional breakdown that was going to take place. I was glad that Tyrone was going to be there with me to help me through this difficult situation. When Tyrone and I walked into Aisha's room, we both stood there in the middle of the floor as if we had walked into the twilight zone. The room appeared to be spinning and I started to feel as if I was going to faint. Tyrone took me by the hand and led me to Aisha's bed. I hadn't been in Aisha's room since the day I had to pick out what I wanted her to be buried in. I remember what I picked out to bring her home from the hospital when she was born. I shouldn't have had to pick out the last outfit that my child would ever wear. I agree with Denzel Washington in the movie,

*John Q.* No parent should have to bury their child; our children should bury us.

"Maybe you should sit down before we start packing up Aisha's things," Tyrone said, with watery eyes.

"Yeah, because I feel like I am going to pass out."

I still couldn't believe that my child is gone. How is a parent really supposed to move on after burying their child? This is the kind of thing that I would see on the news but it never really dawned on me that this could happen to me.

I decided to pack up Aisha's clothes and shoes first because I was going to give them to a homeless shelter for women. I didn't want to give them to the Salvation Army, although that is a good cause. I didn't want to give her things away to be sold; instead, I wanted to give them away to someone in need without them having to purchase the items.

After Aisha's clothes and shoes were packed, I began packing her books and I came across her diary. I placed the diary in the box with the other mementos I was planning to keep as memory of my daughter. I was really going to miss her. She was more than a daughter. Aisha was my friend. I know some people don't think that parents should be friends with their kids but I disagree. Aisha and I had a very unique mother-daughter relationship. While most girls her age were hanging at the mall with their friends, she would call me at work and say, "Mom, how about we go on a shopping spree and have a girl's day this weekend?" Girl's day included getting our hair and nails done. We would sometimes even go the make up counter at the department store and have the make up artists do our faces like supermodels. I was a young mother so many people didn't know right away that I was Aisha's mother. It bothered me at first that

*When I'm Loving You*

people thought we were sisters, but I learned to accept it as a compliment.

We were almost finished packing Aisha's room when Tyrone began to cry. He was holding a photo album of pictures of Aisha and her friends. I was in many of the photos as well. He appeared to realize all that he missed not being in Aisha's daily life.

"I'm so sorry I wasn't here for you and Aisha," Tyrone said, while trying to hold back more tears.

"Tyrone, I know. It's okay. We both made some bad decisions but we can't continue to dwell on them. This is going to be tough for us I know because we have lost our child. I'm not sure how we are supposed to manage Ty but we are going to have to help each other cope."

Tyrone look at me with such a surprised look on his face. "You called me Ty. You haven't called me that since Aisha was about two or three years old."

He was right. I started calling him Tyrone after we broke up. Ty was more of my pet name for him and after we went our separate ways, Tyrone was more appropriate.

It was getting late so Tyrone and I decided to finish the remainder of Aisha's room the next day after I go to brunch with Dianne and Lynda. It was our ritual for the first Sunday of each month, getting together and catching up on each other's lives. Tyrone had checked out of the hotel since I told him he could stay with me until he went back to Georgia. He was going to sleep on the sofa, but I really didn't want to be alone. I really wanted him to make love to me again, but I wasn't sure if he was going to be in the mood since he had a breakdown while helping me pack Aisha's things. He was finally allowing himself to grieve over the loss of Aisha.

When we climbed into bed, Tyrone started to cry again. He was carrying so much guilt around with him, but I somehow wanted him to let it go. However, I knew he would have to get though it at his own pace. I let him grieve for our daughter and I held him and kept reminding him that we were going to get through this together. Consoling Tyrone led into a night of passionate lovemaking. It felt so good to have him inside of me once again. I wasn't sure how long this was going to last but I decided to enjoy every minute of it while it lasted. After all, I still loved Tyrone, always have and probably always will.

The next morning when we woke up, Tyrone looked like he didn't get much sleep at all.

"Did you get any sleep last night Ty?"

"Not much, but I will try to get some rest while you are at brunch with Dianne and Lynda. By the way, how are they doing?"

"They are doing well, but I will get the updates on what's been going on in their lives today."

"Are you going to tell them about us?"

"Probably so. Why, you don't want me to?"

"No, it's cool. I was wondering what you ladies talk about. Tell them I said hello."

"I sure will."

I kissed Tyrone on the forehead and then headed for the shower. He looked so exhausted, but he had several hours to sleep before it would be time to finish Aisha's room. While I was taking my shower, it dawned on me that Tyrone and I didn't use a condom so I immediately started to worry. Although I loved Tyrone, now was not the time to risk pregnancy, a sexually transmitted disease or worse.

## CHAPTER 5

# JASPER'S

**IT WAS A BEAUTIFUL SUNDAY MORNING,** perfect for brunch with the girls. Lynda, Dianne and I usually meet at least one Sunday a month at 11:00 a.m. at Jaspers in Greenbelt, MD for brunch. In my opinion, Jaspers have the best all you can eat brunch buffet in Prince George's County. I was so happy about Tyrone and I trying to work things out I couldn't wait to share the news with my best friends. I really hope Dianne does not try to over analyze the situation because I'm really not in the mood for it today.

We all pulled up in the parking lot of Jaspers within a couple of minutes of each other. Punctuality was very important to us. That's one thing that we all had in common. Lynda was looking fly as always and Dianne was all business-like. I don't know why she has to look professional even on the weekends, but that's Dianne. Once we were seated at our table, we headed for the buffet to fill our plates with fruit, waffles, eggs, bacon; you name it. I couldn't wait to share my news so I immediately started talking once we were back at our table.

"Y'all would never guess who I bumped into Friday."

"Bumped into? I thought you were supposed to be home packing," Dianne remarked as if she was my mother.

"Well, not bumped into, but guess who came to visit me?" I rephrased my question.

"Who?" Lynda asked as if she knew this was going to be a juicy story.

"Aisha's dad," I answered, not sure, how they would respond.

"Get outta here," Lynda said all loud and laughing while a piece of her eggs fell out of her mouth. "How did that happen? I mean details girl details."

"Okay, calm down." I couldn't help but laugh at her eagerness to hear the story.

"Well, Tyrone called and said he was in town on business and he really wanted to talk to me. Since I blew him off at the funeral, I figured I would at least give him a chance to say whatever was on his mind. I guess he needed closure."

"Yeah, go on," Dianne snapped.

As I continued my story, I could tell that Dianne was not as eager to hear this story as Lynda was. "So I told him to come on over since I was still packing up my things. When he got there he handed me an envelope, kiss me on the check and left. Inside the envelope were a letter and banking information for the account he opened for Aisha several years ago."

"How much was in the account?" Lynda asked.

*When I'm Loving You*

"Dag Lynda, chill. Let her finish the story," Dianne snapped.

"Alright, my bad."

"Anyway, after reading the letter he wrote, I needed to see him, you know, so I could get some things off my chest. So I went to his hotel room, we talked, and then one thing led to another and—"

"You fucked Tyrone?" Lynda interjected.

Dianne looked at me for confirmation. There was a silence at the table for a few seconds before I responded. "I sure did."

"What?" Dianne asked sounding disgusted.

"Yes I did Dianne, my goodness!"

"Was it good?" Lynda asked as if we were teenagers experiencing sex for the first time.

"It sure was," I responded giving her a hi-five.

"So you had a one-night stand with Tyrone, isn't he married?" Dianne asked with her arms folded.

"Nope, not anymore."

"Did you know that before or after y'all had sex?"

"Why Dianne, damn?"

"I was *only* asking."

"No, you were *only* judging and I'm tired of it."

"Well excuse me, I won't ask you anything else about Tyrone then. I'm concerned about you, that's all. Sorry for being a friend."

"I don't mind you being a friend, but I'm tired of you trying to be my shrink. I'm okay. I'm a big girl if you haven't noticed.

"Well excuse me Ms. I'm a big girl. If my memory serves me correctly, I was the one who was up with you all night on the phone when Tyrone wouldn't act right Natasha. I remember how he hurt you when he started running the streets and coming home drunk and high all the time. I flew to Georgia to help you pack so you can move away from him. I'm not saying people can't change Natasha, but be careful."

"Dianne, I know you are my friend and you mean well, but you act like Nelson is the only man who is decent. He's not perfect either."

"What does Nelson have to do with what I'm saying? Tyrone hurt you and you're sitting there acting like he didn't. There is no excuse for how he treated you, but hey, it's not for me to decide. When he starts acting up again, I really don't want to hear about it."

"I can't believe you Dianne."

"No I can't believe you. After all he's put you through."

"Dianne, I still love him. I never stopped." I could feel myself beginning to cry. "And if you can't be happy that we are trying to work things out then so be it. I need him right now in a way that no one else can be there for me. No matter what, we created a life together, Aisha, and we lost her. She's gone and I need him in my life right now. It may not be forever, none of us know that, but I need him right now."

I placed the money for my food on the table and left the restaurant. I couldn't sit there another minute defending how I feel. I don't owe anyone an explanation on what I choose to do with my life or whom I choose to spend it with. I know Dianne has been there for me through some hard times, but she doesn't have the time anymore to be there the way I need her to be. She has Nelson so why can't I have Tyrone, even if it's only temporary?

## Chapter 6

# The Apology

**NATASHA WAS RIGHT,** she is a big girl and able to make her own decisions. I've had to come to her rescue so many times that I often felt the need to protect her. But as her friend, if she wants me to back off then I need to do that. Natasha is going through so much hurt right now that I didn't want her to be making this decision to be with Tyrone because they have lost Aisha.

Aisha meant a lot to me as well. She was my goddaughter and we were very close. I can't even begin to imagine what it must be like to lose a child because it's hard enough dealing with it as a godmother. After talking to Nelson about what happened at Jaspers, he told me that I was wrong and I needed to apologize to Natasha. I was mad at him at first, but I knew he was right. I wish I could take some of the pain off Natasha because she has already been through so much with the lost of her parents, being a teenage mom, and now losing her daughter. At the same time, I admire her for being so strong. No matter what she has been through, she has always managed to pick up the pieces and move on with her life.

Natasha is an only child and so were both of her parents. She didn't have much family so when she lost her parents, she lost everything even her spirit. That's how we became friends. I would see her crying in the bathroom between classes so I would stay and talk to her. I would miss my own classes, if Natasha didn't feel up to going to her class. I was suspended for missing so many of my classes. After we explained the situation to the guidance counselor, he gave both of us a chance to make up all of our missed work. It was on Saturdays, but I didn't care. Natasha was my new best friend and I promised to always be there for her.

She was always so sad after her parents died because with no aunts or uncles, she was put in foster care. She was well taken care of; her foster mother was a friend of her parents. She would always say that she felt so empty inside. It wasn't until she met Tyrone that joy was brought back into her life. I was so happy that she found someone to love unconditionally and who loved her the same way. What I loved about Tyrone back then was that he was genuinely concerned about her. She told me that he didn't try to have sex with her or take advantage of her vulnerability. She actually had to initiate sex with him their first time together. Unfortunately, the streets became more important to him and he was completely out of control once his mother died.

Natasha was always so beautiful inside and out and people thought her life must be great. She was very popular in high

*When I'm Loving You*

school because not only was she beautiful, she was also smart and talented. In our senior year, she was voted most attractive, most talented, and she was prom queen. I was only voted most likely to succeed, but I didn't hate on her. She could sing her ass off. She never wanted to pursue a singer career though because of what women normally have to go through to be accepted in the music industry. And Natasha wasn't about to sleep her way to get anything. Above all, she had a great personality and she still does.

I worried about her after I moved to Maryland not that long after graduation. I had plenty of family in the area, so the transition was easy for me. However, it wasn't too long after I moved when Natasha moved to Maryland. We've been friends for so long. I hope I didn't ruin our friendship with my insensitivity. I was beginning to feel terrible about my conversation with Natasha and she wasn't taking any of my calls. Lynda said that she hadn't heard from her either. I was so worried about her that I decided to go over to her new condominium. I haven't been over there yet because she moved shortly after our disagreement.

When I reached Natasha's place, her car wasn't outside, so I didn't think anyone was home. I decided to write her a note and leave it in her mailbox. As I approached the mailbox, her door opened. It was Tyrone.

"Hey there Princess Di, what's up girl?" Tyrone said, with a boyish tone. That's what they called me in high school.

"Hey Tyrone, I'm doing very well. How are you?"

"I'm maintaining."

"I wanted to leave a note for Natasha to call me. I know she is probably upset with me so I wanted to apologize to her for being so insensitive. Tyrone, I don't want to get into your business but I am concerned."

"Dianne, I know why you must be concerned but I love Natasha and you know that. I never meant to hurt her in any way. Remember Natasha left me and kept Aisha from me. I tried to see her, I tried to send her money but after a while, I was tired of being rejected. I got married so I could move on with my life, but I never stopped loving Natasha or my daughter."

"I know Tyrone and I'm sorry. Of course, I only remember how hurt she was when things didn't work out and no, I don't know your side of the story. I do understand that it really isn't my business but I was the one she always called when you weren't there. So you can't blame me for worrying."

"Trust me, Natasha appreciates they way you care about her. Although she is a grown woman, she has always respected your opinion. You are more like a sister to her. She is very upset about what happened at brunch that day. She didn't get into any details, but I know it was about her getting back with me."

"Are you getting back together?"

"I am going to be here for Natasha as long as she wants me here. I was going to go back to Georgia but my job said they could find me an assignment here. I love her and I don't want her to go through this alone."

"What about you Tyrone, how are you holding up?"

"Like I said, I'm maintaining. It's hard and I feel so bad because I wasn't here for them. I can't make up for those years but I'm here now for as long as Natasha wants to be bothered."

"Well, I am glad to hear that. I can't say that I am not worried but if you mean what you are saying then she is in good hands."

*When I'm Loving You*

"Yeah, she is. Other than my mother, Natasha is the only woman I have ever loved unconditionally. I can't even say that about my ex-wife. She was just convenient. I know that's not a reason to marry someone, but I was a broken man when Natasha left with our daughter. Then my mother died. I needed someone, but Natasha always had my heart."

"Where is she anyway?" I finally asked.

"She went to get her hair and nails done. She also mentioned getting a massage. She needed a day of pampering."

"Please let her know I was here and to call me when she feels like talking. Tell her that I love her and I am sorry. I only want to see her happy and I see that she is happy with you."

"Thanks, Dianne. She'll appreciate that."

I was actually smiling on my way home. There is no doubt in my mind that Tyrone loves Natasha but I hope he is ready to be there for her the way she needs a man to be there. I will stay out of their situation but I will cut a brotha if I have to.

# Six Months Later

## Chapter 7

# Heaven

**TODAY IS THE FIRST DAY** of this self-publishing course I've decided to take in order to help me prepare for publishing my first book. I'm so excited and overwhelmed at the same time because this has been a bittersweet journey. Writing is definitely my passion, but putting this all together for publishing is more of a business venture. Working at the fitness center and chasing Taye has definitely set my schedule back about six months, but it has definitely been worth it. Taye is wonderful and I am glad that we've had this time together, but things for us are starting to become too much of a routine. I need excitement in my life and it feels like Taye and I are growing apart already.

I have been exclusively seeing Taye for about six months now, and all we managed to do was fuck and go to lunch occasionally. I was beginning to think that maybe Taye wasn't that into me. I shouldn't have to dictate to a man what to do to romance me. Maybe there was another woman that he was romancing. Well at this point, it really didn't matter because I was moving on although he didn't know it yet. I even stopped working at the fitness center. My excuse was that I needed the time to dedicate to finishing my book. Although I really wanted us to work out, I decided to allow things to flow in whichever direction they were going to flow.

    I don't know why I was nervous about my first day of class. You would have thought that it was my first day of high school all over again. At thirty-four, sitting in a classroom felt really weird. As I looked around the room, I noticed others were as uncomfortable with the situation. I closed my eyes and took a deep breath and when I opened my eyes, I couldn't believe the energy that was coming from my immediate left. Somewhere between my deep breaths, Zion walked in and took a seat next to me. I haven't seen Zion in years and all of a sudden, high school feelings were brought back to surface. I didn't know Zion personally back in high school, but I knew he was an aspiring writer. He was one of the editors of the school newspaper and he was very popular. I was a couple of grades ahead of him so we didn't have much interaction in school. I am feeling distracted already so I really could use Dianne here with me today to keep me focused in this class.

    When Zion sat down he immediately start asking me questions. The class wasn't scheduled to start until 6:00 p.m. and it was only 5:45 p.m. *Was this going to be a long fifteen minutes or what?* From my peripheral, I could feel him looking at me.

    "You look familiar," Zion said, not hesitating to start a conversation.

## When I'm Loving You

"I believe we went to the same high school." I said, trying not to look directly at him.

The chemistry between us was too much for me and several times, I considered leaving the class. Zion came up with a series of other questions to ask me and I answered each one of them trying not to show that I was attracted to him. Little did he know, in my mind I had already pictured him naked. I haven't felt this kind of chemistry from a man in a long time, not even from Taye.

At the end of the class, I tried to hurry out of the room, but of course, Zion caught up with me to start another conversation. Couldn't he see that I was trying to get away from him?

"What's your hurry?"

"It's been a long day and I'm ready to go home."

"The night is still young though."

"Not for us old-heads."

"Old-head? Please. How old are you?"

"Excuse me?"

"Oh, I forgot. I'm not supposed to ask a lady her age."

"That's right, but anyway I'm thirty-four. When I was in the twelfth grade, you were in the tenth so I believe so that makes you thirty-two."

"Exactly and wow, you look great."

"Thanks!"

"So home is really your destination huh?"

"Yep."

"Nothing I can do to change your mind?"

"Why, what do you have in mind?" I asked assuming he was like most of the men I met, trying to get me alone so they could be close to the panties.

"Are you hungry? I know I could use something to eat. It's only a little after eight o'clock, so it's not too late for dinner. My treat, so how about it? You down?"

I really wanted to say no, but I couldn't. He is too darn sexy.

"Sure, why not." For a moment, I actually forgot about Taye.

Zion and I went to eat at a nearby spot around the corner from where the class was being held. This was too much for me already and I couldn't get a hold of my emotions. I didn't know what I was feeling at the moment but it was a great feeling. Over dinner, we conversed about so many things. It was amazing that we had so much in common. We both loved movies, bowling, reading books, and skating. I haven't met a guy in years that would still go skating so I was really excited about getting to know more about him. We discussed the books we were preparing to publish and our love for art, music and poetry. I could talk to him for hours, and to think, I was trying to elude him after class. He was a serious breath of fresh air for me and I couldn't get enough.

"So have you written anything other than your book?"

"Yes, as a matter of fact I've written several poems."

"Really, I would love to hear them some day if you don't mind."

"No, I would love to recite them for you. It would be my pleasure."

"I can't wait."

"Well I recite poetry at different spoken word events and you are more than welcome to come out and hear me. Let me know when you want to do that."

"That sounds wonderful," I responded like a little girl on Christmas.

That night when I arrived home, I quickly showered and headed for bed. Thoughts of Zion were in my head and they were explicit thoughts. I imagined him slowly undressing me and caressing my body. I imagined how it would feel if he kissed every inch of me but concentrating on my breasts and my pussy. I imagined him licking and gently sucking on my clit as he held my legs that were constantly trembling. I felt myself getting wet thinking about it so I decided to touch myself to help the visual in my mind. I really can't believe this guy has me masturbating after only spending a few hours with him. All I can say is Taye better step up his game, big-time!

I met Taye the next day for lunch. He could tell that I was distracted but he never asks too many questions. That is one thing that I especially liked about Taye. I never felt pressured about anything. I didn't know how to tell Taye that I was actually bored with our relationship and that it was no longer exciting. The things we did became too much of a routine for me. I needed some spontaneity. I'm glad that I have Zion to think about because when new relationships didn't work out, I would always run back to whatever Maurice had to offer. Normally that was only sex, sex, and more sex. I'm actually bored with that too.

When I returned to the office, I had an email from Zion. I was so excited. The subject of the email was "Let's Talk Poetry." I couldn't wait to read the contents of the email. It read:

*Let's talk poetry your place or mine*
*Burn incense and candles*
*Pour a couple of glasses of wine*

# K. Lowery Moore

*Take our shoes off and relax massage each other's mind*
*I say one line and you say the first thing*
*That comes to your mind*

That made me smile. I've always loved writing poetry but lately I have been consumed with writing my book. I decided to respond to his email with a little poetry of my own, with some added flirting of course.

*Okay, let's talk poetry but while I straddle you*
*I would love to talk poetry because I am feeling you*
*A man that's not afraid to express what's he's feeling*
*I'm impressed*
*I wanna talk poetry but after we undress*

We continued to flirt by email for about the next ten minutes and then Zion finally asked me out on a date. He said that he wanted to take me to a poetry reading on Friday night and then if time allowed we'd catch a movie. All week long, I anticipated my first date with Zion. I was beyond excited.

∽ ∽ ∽ ∽ ∽

Friday night arrived and the long anticipated wait to see Zion was over. It was an unseasonably warm spring night. He picked me up and we headed to the poetry spot. The ambiance was perfect for reciting poetry. The club was dimly lit creating a romantic atmosphere. Zion recited a poem and I am not going to lie, I don't know what he was saying. I was too busy imagining him naked and making love to me. When the host asked if anyone

## When I'm Loving You

else wanted to recite something, I built up the nerve to recite a poem that I had written for Zion. I was so nervous but I made it through it. I took a deep breath and recited:

*I've been wondering*
*What it would be like to be close to you*
*Just the two of us face to face alone at my place*
*I've been fantasizing about*
*What it would be like to straddle you*
*Look into your eyes, kiss you softly*
*First on your lips, then on your neck, then on your chest*
*And don't worry for you I won't neglect the rest*
*I also want you to explore my body*
*Every inch of me, slowly, show me how you do*
*Because I am so into you*
*So I've been wondering*
*What it would be like for you to be in me*
*Stroking deeply, damn freak me baby on my silk sheets*
*Tasting me will be a treat*
*Don't you know how well chocolate goes with caramel?*
*So I was wondering*
*Are you up for a game of show and tell?*
*Yeah, you're up*
*And I can show you better than I can tell you*
*What I've been wanting to do to you!*

After I recited the poem, some of the couples who were there held each other close and other couples kissed passionately. Zion looked at me as if he could have sexed me right there with everyone in the room. I guess he couldn't

83

take it anymore because no sooner than I sat down, he asked if I was ready to leave. We had only been there for about an hour.

ഔ ഔ ഔ ഔ ഔ

When we left the poetry reading, we held hands as we walked to his car. As we approached his car, he stopped and kissed me. It was such a passionate kiss, wet but not too sloppy. Zion was about to open the passenger side of the door when he leaned me up against the car door instead. I wasn't sure what he was about to do but I was excited. Zion then hugged me as if he had no plans of ever letting me go. I could tell by his erection that he was turned on. Perhaps my poem did the trick. I moved in closer to him so I could get a better feel of his erection. I knew it wasn't the best thing to do if we were going to catch the movie, however, I decided to go along with the moment.

"Was that poem for me?" he asked, in that sexy voice of his.

"*Yes*" was all I could manage to say. It felt so good in his arms that I didn't want him to let me go, ever! I kissed him on the neck to let him know that it was okay to continue holding me.

"Do you still want to go to the movies?" I asked hoping he would say no.

"It's up to you," he responded with the cutest smirk.

Before I could answer him, he reached his hand under my skirt and slipped his finger in my panties. I was somewhat surprised by his forwardness but yet excited at the same time.

*When I'm Loving You*

"It appears that you don't want to go to the movies," Zion whispered to me as he felt my wetness. "Tell me why your pussy is so wet." *Same reason why your dick is so hard*, I thought to myself.

I really didn't know what to say so I gave him a soft kiss on his lips and looked him in his eyes. We stared into each other's eyes before he started kissing me again with his wet but not so sloppy style. For a moment, I forgot that we were outside. He backed me up to the car and then bent down on his knees.

"Zion, what are you doing? We're outside."

Zion didn't respond. He looked around to see if anyone was near. He then pulled down my panties and lifted my right leg out leaving them around my left ankle. He put my right leg on his shoulder. He started licking my clit like he did in my fantasy, but in my fantasy we were not outside. "Come on Zion, stop," I said, as I moaned and grabbed the back of his head. Isn't it funny how we ask someone to stop, but pull them close at the same time? He slid his finger inside of me while his tongue was still making friends with my clit. I felt my legs shaking and I could barely stand on one leg.

"Zion I think someone is coming," I said to him when I thought I heard voices. But what I should have said was *Zion I'm cumming.*

Zion then moved my leg and made sure my skirt was down. Before he stood, he took my panties from around my left ankle and shoved them into his pocket. That was telling me that this session was not over. Once we were inside the car, he leaned my seat back. I knew he had something freaky in mind so I didn't even question what he was doing. *Thank goodness, his windows are tinted* I thought to myself. For a moment, Zion stroked his erection through his jeans. He was probably wondering if he had any condoms on him.

Because I didn't want the first time we made love to be in a car, I decided to return the favor he gave me. I reached over, unbuttoned, and unzipped his jeans. Obviously excited, he didn't waste anytime pulling down his pants enough so I could pull out his erection. I started giving him stroking the shaft of his penis and teasing his opening with my tongue. I recommend that any women interested in pleasing a man orally should stick their tongue in this opening. The first guy I tried that with lifted up and pulled an almost exorcist move. I knew that dude was about to levitate off the bed. It startled me until I realize that he was on his way to the most explosive oral orgasm I've ever seen a man have.

As Zion moaned, I wondered what his dick looked like but it was too dark inside the car for me to see it the way I wanted to see it. Then he whispered the magic words as he ran his fingers through my hair, "Let's go back to your house." I gently stroked Zion's dick during the fifteen-minute drive to my house. His erection subsided a little which I was glad. I didn't want to create a mess in his car with his semen nor was I quite comfortable with swallowing if you know what I mean.

When we reached the front door of my house, we barely made it inside the door before Zion took off my clothes and laid me down on my living room floor. He looked me over as if he was trying to figure out what to do to me next. Almost like an animal looking over his prey. He must have figured it out because he picked me up and sat me on my dinning room table. It's obvious that he is not a conventional brotha. After pulling a condom from his pocket, he took off his clothes and put the rubber on his penis.

## When I'm Loving You

*Okay so he had a condom, so I wonder what he was thinking to himself in the car before I showed my oral skills.* I watched his hand slowly pull the rubber up on his approximately nine-inch erection. *Damn his dick is beautiful—nice length, impressive width, and perfectly circumcised. I'll thank his mama later,* I thought to myself as I admired his body. As he walked up to me, I took a deep breath and bit my bottom lip.

"What's wrong baby?"

"Nothing," I answered nervously.

"Are you sure?"

"Yes I'm sure," I answered him trying to hide the fact that I was nervous.

Zion eased himself into me and all I could do was moan and lay back on the table. It wasn't the most romantic moment but the passion was incredible. He moved inside of me as if he was making sure he touched every inch of me. It felt so good I wanted to scream. After a few more thrusts, he lifted me off the table and I wrapped my legs around his waist so his dick would stay inside of me.

"Can we go to your bedroom? You feel so good. I want to really get up in you."

"Sure. No objections here."

Inside my bedroom, he laid me down on the bed and we had sex in every position imaginable. It was indescribable. I must admit sex with Taye is good, but with Zion there is so much more passion and excitement. We made love, sexed, and fucked as if we were becoming one all in one night. With each thrust from Zion, I would moan, call his name and beg for more. *"Ooooh Zion, please don't stop. Keep it right there."* He gave me more than I could have asked for that night.

My first night with Zion was amazing. Although I was flirting with him, sex wasn't really on my agenda because I thought it was too soon. However, I knew it was inevitable considering the chemistry between us. I was in Heaven.

The next morning, Zion could tell that I was a bit withdrawn. He asked me a series of questions, which suggested to me that he was concerned that he didn't please me. I assured him that I was very much so pleased but that we needed to talk.

"Zion, we probably should have had this conversation before we had sex, but I guess now would be as appropriate."

He looked down at the floor as if he knew where I was going with the conversation.

"We didn't talk about our status and Zion I do have a friend who is very special to me. We are not in a committed relationship but we have been seeing each other for about six months now."

"Seeing each other how?" he asked as if he couldn't believe what he was hearing.

"We've been getting to know each other and now we are at the point to see where our relationship is going."

"Well, where is it going?"

"I'm not sure Zion."

He seemed so disgusted with me. I couldn't handle the look on his face so I started to cry.

"What are you crying for? You are the one who hit me with this news. I don't understand why you are so upset. If anyone should be upset it should be me."

"Please don't be angry with me Zion."

"How am I supposed to feel, tell me how you want me to feel?"

"I'm so sorry. Zion, I don't want us to stop seeing each other."

*When I'm Loving You*

I wish I could have read his mind at that moment, because the nostalgic look on his face suggested to me that there was something that he also needed to confess something. Instead, he lay back on the bed and pulled me into his arms. We held each other until we drifted off to sleep. When I woke up, Zion was gone. He left a note on my nightstand that simply said, *Maybe this is too much for both of us right now. We'll talk soon though.* I couldn't believe what I was reading but I certainly wasn't a stranger to heartbreak.

The next few class sessions were very awkward for me. Zion would come into the classroom and sit in the back. He wouldn't even look in my direction. I felt so rejected but it wasn't his fault. I couldn't take the silent treatment from Zion anymore so I didn't make it to the rest of the classes. I told the instructor I was sick and wasn't sure if I would continue with the class. I could register for another session later. He must have shared this with the rest of the class for some reason because Zion sent me a text message asking why I wasn't going to return to class. I simply didn't respond. Why? All he was doing for the past few weeks was ignoring me.

I needed to clear my thoughts of Zion and, seeing him week after week, for five more weeks wasn't going to help. I also told Taye that I needed a break from our situation as well. He must have felt the same way because he didn't ask any questions. He said, "okay" and told me to "take care and good luck with publishing your book." His response was so cold and unfeeling. All I could do was cry.

I know I did the right thing by breaking things off with Taye. I was so drawn to Zion that he was all I could think about, but I'm sure I ruined the chance of us getting to know each other better. Trying to forget Zion, I ran back to Maurice. I didn't learn my lesson with messing around with Maurice until one abortion later. I must have gotten pregnant during our sexual episode in the restroom at his job. That's the only time I can remember not using any protection. I went there for comfort, but as usual he gave me sex and I left with his seed. I had the abortion alone; I didn't tell Natasha or Dianne. I didn't even mention to Maurice that I was pregnant with his child. After the abortion, I slipped into a depression and I would cry myself to sleep every night for weeks. I was so tired of being lonely. Even if you have someone is your bed every night your heart can still be lonely, trust me I know and I was ready to turn that around. I wasn't sure how. I felt like I went from being in heaven to living in hell.

## Chapter 8

# Phone Call

"**WHO IS CALLING ME** in the middle of the day?" I asked aloud as the phone startled me out of my afternoon nap. "Who in the hell knows that I am home today?" Normally I would be at work at this time but I decided to call in sick, since it was almost a year, to the day, when I buried my daughter.

"Hello," I answered the phone with a slight attitude especially since I didn't recognize the telephone number.

"Is this Natasha Inglewood?"

"May I ask who is calling?"

"Is this Natasha?"

"Yes, who is this?" I snapped.

"Well, this is Annie."

"Who?"

"Bitch don't act you don't know who this is."

"Bitch? I got your bitch if you call my house again. You do know phone numbers can be traced. You must don't know about Google.com, you simple ass bitch." I was so pissed off as I slammed the phone down. I managed to get back into my nap. The phone rang again.

"Hello. What do you want?" I yelled into the phone noticing it was the same number.

"What do I want? I want my husband back," The person on the other end said, before she hung up.

That's when it clicked. This was Tyrone's ex-wife Angelica. Shit I didn't know they called her Annie. "Why is she calling me?"

I decided not to tell Tyrone that Angelica called because I really thought this was going to be an isolated incident. I could not have been more wrong.

It was a Friday night, the girls' night out. I was meeting Lynda and Dianne for drinks at 7:00 p.m. It was our first outing since the brunch incident about six months ago. I missed hanging out with the girls. There was so much going on in our personal lives these days that we hadn't really had a chance to get together. Dianne and I were on speaking terms again and I was glad. When I walked out of Jaspers that day, I didn't intend for to stop speaking. However, I needed some time to get my thoughts together. She had a few good points but I really wanted her to understand that I still loved Tyrone. I respected her opinion but, in no way, did I need her approval on anything I did. I love her dearly so I'm glad that we were able to move past our disagreement.

I was ready to get my party on. We like to get to the club while drinks are half price. Getting off work at 5:00 p.m., I wanted to run home for a quick shower. When I pulled up to my condo, I noticed a car parked out in front of the building with Georgia tags. Something didn't feel right so I called Dianne on her cell phone but her answer machine came on.

"Hey Dianne, this is Natasha. Girl, call me as soon as you get this message. It's a car in front of my building with some female in it and I don't know why anyone would be outside in one of my parking spaces, especially with Georgia tags. So, call me as soon as you get this message."

That's when it hit me that this might be Tyrone's ex-wife. Who else could it be? That explains the strange calls.

"Hello," I said answering my cell phone.

"Hey girl, this is Di. I got your message. What is going on?"

"I have no idea, but I have a feeling something is about to go down with Tyrone's ex-wife."

"Well, where is Tyrone?"

"He's probably on his way home from work. You know he's probably having some fellas over for the basketball game tonight since we were supposed to be hanging out tonight. Hold on Dianne, my other line is beeping."

"It's about to be a what, girl fight," It was Lynda singing that song I can't stand by some singer name Brooke Valentine. Who is she anyway?

"Girl, ain't nobody fighting, you are so crazy," I said, laughing at her.

"Hey, either way I'm on my way to your house."

"Damn, why Dianne call you? You always ready to fight somebody."

"You know how we roll. Birds of a feather."

"Yeah, well let's hope this is not her outside my house or if it is her, that she comes correct. Oh shoot, Dianne is still on the other line. I'll see you when you get here. And please leave the camouflage and heavy artillery at home. I don't think you will need it, G. I. Lynda."

"Whateva!" Lynda said, as she hung up.

"Dianne, you still there?" I asked clicking back over to my other line.

"Yes, was that Tyrone?"

"Naw, it was Lynda's crazy ass. She's going to meet me here. Why did you call her? You know how she is. Remember that time she was about to kill that waitress in Outback, in Rivertown Shopping Center, until we convinced her that minimum wage bitch wasn't worth risking her freedom over. Her temper scares me sometimes," I said, laughing but I was also serious.

"Lord, let me come over there to keep everything civil."

"Yes Mrs. Freud. We'll be right here so you can come analyze this situation."

"Forget you. I'm on my way. I hope I make it before Lynda, now that I think about it. That Outback incident was a couple of years ago, but she might get a flashback. Make sure you call Tyrone on his cell phone just in case. Bye."

*She's so bossy, but so right*, I thought as I dialed Tyrone's cell phone number. When I told him about our unexpected visitor, he asked me to stay in my car until he arrive; he was about five minutes away. That was the longest five minutes. I was wondering why the woman never approached my car, but then I realized she has never seen me before in person, only pictures of me when I was younger. As soon as Tyrone pulled up in front of the house, he started going off so that must be Annie.

When he got out of the car, she did too. They were arguing about something so, of course, I couldn't sit in the car any longer.

As I walked closer, Annie looked at me and started yelling at Tyrone. "Is this her? Is this the woman you couldn't get over all these years? The one who is all this, and all that. The woman you compared me with constantly. Well she doesn't look like much."

"What the fuck did you say?" I asked, as I approached them.

"You heard me, you don't look like much."

"Did you come all the way to Maryland, from Georgia, to tell me that or is there something else you trying to do?" I stepped up in her face.

Tyrone stepped in between us. "Natasha baby, please just go in the house."

"Yeah bitch, go inside," Annie said, with a smirk.

I lunged at her, but Tyrone caught me. "Natasha, baby you are better than this so let me handle her."

Just then, Lynda and Dianne pulled up. As they got out of their cars, Tyrone asked them to take me inside but I couldn't let this go. How dare she come all the way here, trying to claim someone that no longer belongs to her? She is the one who filed for divorce, not Tyrone. I guess she didn't understand why he was grieving the loss of a child he barely knew. Regardless, Aisha was his daughter and Annie should have been there for him.

I decided to go inside the house when I heard her say to Tyrone, "So you are going to let your dead daughter come in between what we had?"

Before I knew it, I was all over that woman. I had my hand around her throat promising to kill her if she ever mentioned my daughter again, for any reason. Tyrone had to literally pry my fingers from around her neck. Dianne was yelling for me to come inside my house.

"Natasha girl, get in here before you kill her."

"Well she shouldn't come up here like she's all bad. She doesn't know me. Tell her I will slit her throat if she makes reference to my child ever again."

"I know you will and that's why I want you to come inside. Please! I am not going to be able to bail you out of jail."

"Why not?" I asked confused.

"Because I will be in jail with you, and Lynda too. You know Nelson will leave me right in jail if I get into a fist fight."

"Now you know Nelson would get you from Iraq in the middle of the war," Lynda said, laughing. I cut my eye at her because I didn't feel like laughing, although it was funny.

"Natasha, come inside so you can get dressed to go."

"I'm not in the mood anymore," I said, crying as I walked in the house. Losing my child was bad enough, but now I have to deal with the crazy ex-wife of my child's father. Drama! Why can't women let it go when a man makes it clear that he doesn't want them anymore? I love Tyrone, but I can't go through this. I can't stand drama. That's why I didn't put up a fight years ago when he started running the streets. It's not worth all of that. I let him go, even though I loved him. I wanted to avoid drama and now drama has found me anyway.

A few of Tyrone's boys came over, but he didn't want to watch the game. He thought we needed to talk about what

*When I'm Loving You*

happened with Annie. I told Tyrone to allow the fellas to stay; I wanted to go to bed. Before I climbed into bed, he told me there was no doubt in his mind that he was where he wanted to be. A part of me wanted him to leave me alone, but I love Tyrone. He held me while I cried myself to sleep. It hurt so badly not to have my daughter here. I really don't know how I am going to make it. It is hard to believe Aisha has been gone for about a year.

About two weeks later, after Annie showed up at my place, she had the nerve to call my house again. This time it was to apologize. She was trying to explain that she was hurt and she wasn't thinking clearly. That's how some people get killed and other people go to jail, not thinking.

## Chapter 9
## News

**I FELT GOOD** after I had a chance to talk to Tyrone about what's been on my mind regarding him and Natasha. I know that I have to let them work out their own situation, but I'm glad I was able to get how I felt off my chest.

It seems like Tyrone is not the one I might have to cut, instead it may be his ex-wife. Nothing has happened since the day she showed up outside of Natasha's condominium. However, I make sure Natasha always know that I have her back, no matter what. Lately, Natasha seemed so happy with Tyrone and, of course, it makes me happy to see the people I care about happy.

I was in an extremely good mood so I decided to surprise Nelson with a night of extreme passion. It's been a while since I did a striptease number for him, so I thought it was time to break out the black lace pumps. Lynda and I took classes to learn how to swing around the pole. I even bought a portable pole so I know Nelson would be especially excited tonight.

When Nelson came home, I was expecting him to come into the family room, as he normally does after a hard day at work. He would come in, sit down on the sofa, and read whatever mail I put on the end table for him. I would even have a cold Corona waiting for him so he can unwind. Today was different. When he came home from work, he went upstairs to our bedroom. I followed behind him. When I came into the room, he had laid back on the bed with his arm over his face. It was evident that something was wrong with my husband.

"Nelson, baby, is everything okay?" I asked as I walked into the room.

"No, Dianne, we need to talk and I've been wondering how I was going to break this to you all day."

"Baby, what's wrong?" I was afraid of his answer because I've seen *Waiting to Exhale. Please don't be leaving me,* I thought to myself as I lay down beside him. *And especially not for a white woman or, Lord help me, a man.* I rolled over on top of Nelson. He ran his fingers through my hair and looked in to my eyes.

"Dianne, you know I love you and there is nothing I wouldn't do for you. I would never do anything to intentionally hurt you. There is no easy way to tell you this but I just found out that I have a daughter."

At that moment, my world shattered.

"What? You cheated on me, Nelson?" I asked as I cried harder than I've cried in a long time.

## When I'm Loving You

"No, baby, no I didn't cheat on you. She's eleven."

"Huh?" I couldn't control my tears. A part of me was glad that he wasn't coming out of the closet or leaving me, but this was too much for me to handle.

"Apparently, my ex-girlfriend, Marie wasn't only involved with me. When she got pregnant, she told me the baby wasn't mine and I believed her. I was young and I didn't question it. I was relieved that she said it wasn't mine because I wasn't ready to be a father."

I sat there in a daze while he explained to me what he found out. At that moment, I really wanted to die. I know something like this shouldn't be so serious. However, my life, as I know it, is about to change drastically. I didn't bargain for this but I guess this is what comes with "for better or for worse." I don't know if I can handle this.

"How do you know she's actually your daughter?"

"I took a DNA test."

"When, Nelson?" I asked as I jumped off the bed.

"Baby, please calm down. When I got the phone call from Marie, I didn't want to upset you if it wasn't true. So I got the DNA test done and I got the results today."

"What does she want, Nelson?"

"That's the thing Dianne, she doesn't want anything. Marie is dying of leukemia."

"What?"

"That's how this all came about. When she was diagnosed with leukemia, I guess she felt she needed to clear her conscious. Her husband is devastated because not only is he losing his wife, he found out that his little girl is not his child. Now I don't know why he didn't get a blood test back then but this is where we are Dianne."

101

"What is your daughter's name?" I wasn't sure why I asked.

"Nihya," Nelson said, with a little smile.

"That's a beautiful name," was all I could manage to say for a few moments. "Nelson, I am not going to lie to you, this is so hard for me to digest. I just don't know how we are going to proceed from here."

"What do you mean, 'proceed from here,' Dianne?"

"Never mind that now, have you seen Nihya yet?"

"No not yet. Her mother wanted to wait until the DNA results came back first to break the news to her."

"I guess that was a good idea." I walked out of the room. I guess there will be no extreme night of passion tonight.

ع ع ع ع ع

I went down to the family room and packed up my portable pole. The news of Nelson's daughter was so painful. I sat on the floor and cried. I know this must be hard for Nelson but I can't even consider his feelings right now. When we were married, I always imagined my husband and me having our first child together when we were ready to start a family. I guess this can't happen now. Nelson already has a child.

I love my husband but I don't know if the fact he has a daughter now is going to put a strain on our relationship. On the other hand, it is really sad that Nihya is losing her mother. Unfortunately, I can relate. I was ten years old when my mother died and it was so painful that I blocked it out of my memory until today. I was outside playing with my friends when the older sister of one of my friends came and told me that she had to take me home. I didn't understand why, but she said that something happened to my mother. My world changed that day on the playground. The pain of losing my mother has resurfaced. I was fortunate enough to have a great stepmother. So, I guess now it's my turn to be a great stepmother. I don't know if I can. I don't know if I even want to.

I know it's selfish of me, but I love having my husband to myself. Now I would have to share him with his daughter because now that he knows about Nihya, he is going to want to be an active participant in her life. I don't know if I can handle this.

I must have fallen asleep on the floor, of the family room, because when I woke up, Nelson was lying down beside me with his arm around my waist. We haven't slept apart since we've been married, except when either one of us was on travel. I really want to make this situation work but I have some serious doubts. I'm going to have to pray on this one.

# Chapter 10

# Drama

**DIANNE ASKED NATASHA AND ME** to meet her for drinks after work. Natasha was still upset over the situation with Tyrone's ex-wife and Dianne was upset about something she wouldn't talk about over the telephone. I was still going through somewhat of a depression since I stopped seeing Taye and since I messed things up with getting to know Zion. I haven't even told Natasha or Dianne about the abortion yet. It was decided that we would meet at my place before going to the club since I live the closest to our party spot.

When Natasha arrived, she was her usual cheerful self. I could tell that she was tired but she always seemed to stay in good spirits. What surprised me was when Dianne showed up. She wasn't her usual bossy self. I could tell that she had been crying and it wasn't like Dianne not to have on any makeup at all. Dianne barely made it in the door before she broke down crying. I didn't know what to do because she is the strong one out of the bunch.

"Dianne, is everything okay?" Natasha asked as her eyes began to water.

"I'm not sure," Dianne responded.

"You want to talk about it?" I asked trying to remain strong for her, as I was in a fragile state myself.

"Well, Nelson found out that he is a father."

"What?" Natasha screamed. I stood there in shock.

"Apparently his ex-girlfriend, Marie, was pregnant when they broke up and she told another guy that the baby was his and now she is dying so she decides to clear her conscious."

"How old is the child?" I asked.

"I think she is eleven," Dianne responded.

We all kind of sat there looking at the floor, not knowing what to say. Nelson and Dianne have a great marriage and I'm not sure how this news is going to affect them.

"I love my husband, but I don't know how to make it through this situation. I am trying to be there for him because he is just so distraught right about now. He needs me but I don't know how to be there for him," Dianne said, trying to hold back her tears.

"Dianne, now you know Nelson is a great husband and a wonderful person overall. I'm sure he understands that this is hard for you but I am hoping that you can work this out somehow," Natasha said, as she wiped her own tears.

"What am I going to do? This was not how it was supposed to happen. Nelson and I were supposed to experience having our first child together."

"Dianne, I know you had it all planned out, how your life is supposed to unfold, but life is not always that simple. Life is just not always as cooperative as we want it to be," I added as I thought about the abortion I had recently. I decided not to mention it to them today because I didn't want to take away from what Dianne was going through.

"Try not to give up on him Di. It's not his fault. He didn't know," Natasha pleaded.

"I know it's not but I just don't know how to cope."

Again, we sat there in silence seemingly trying to figure out what to say next.

"Well, we can have a drink right here and watch a movie if y'all want to. I'm really not in the mood for the club scene anyway," I said, hoping they would agree. They both agreed. We decided to watch a comedy in attempt to cheer ourselves up. Anything romantic or dramatic would have been too emotional for all of us at that moment.

While we were watching the movie, we began reminiscing about the interesting dates we had.

"Hey Dianne, do you know what ever happened to that guy you thought was gay?"

"Who?"

"You know the one who ran the surprise bubble bath for you and then came into the living room and blew bubbles off his finger to seduce you."

"Not to mention with the porno playing on the TV."

We laughed so hard the tears started to fall.

"Girl, I don't know. I don't even remember his name," Dianne said. "That's just how insignificant he was for me."

"But he must have been gay or bisexual because don't any man blow bubbles off his damn finger. That was too much," I said, laughing so hard I could barely speak.

"Hey Lynda, you never told us about the threesome you had a few years ago," Dianne said.

"You sure didn't," Natasha added her two cents.

"Because I was hoping that you would forget," I mumbled knowing they were ready for the details now.

"Well at least tell us who it was with," Natasha said, in anticipation of my juicy story.

"Well, the guy was the male dancer, Long Stroke, we hired for Dianne's bridal shower."

Dianne almost spit out the wine she had in her mouth. "What?"

"Yes, so now you know."

"No, no who was the other female?" Natasha insisted.

"Who said it was another female involved?"

"Lord, I don't think I can handle this story," Dianne replied.

"Naw, I'm kidding. It was Jasmine. That's how I found out that Jasmine was bisexual. The plan was to just fuck him, tag team style, but then I could tell that she had other plans in mind."

"Wow, that's deep!" Natasha replied.

"Wait, you never told me that Jasmine was bisexual. Is that why you stopped speaking to her?"

"Yeah, I stopped speaking to her because instead of her telling me about her sexuality, I guess she was just going to show me."

"What did she do?" Natasha and Dianne asked in unison.

*When I'm Loving You*

"Well, when Long Stroke finished fucking Jasmine doggy-style, it was then my turn for whatever I wanted. You know I like my pussy ate, so I lay on my back awaiting him to do his thing. So I'm lying there with my eyes closed, enjoying how my clit is being licked and how good his tongue feels going in and out of my pussy. I mean I had never had any man put his tongue so far in me before so I was like damn this dude got skills, for real, so I decided to watch him in action. To my utmost surprise, it was not him giving me this pleasure, it was Jasmine."

"Oh shit!" Dianne said, sharply.

"Y'all don't know. I could have beaten that bitch's ass right there. It was wild to me because it felt so good I started questioning my own sexuality. I know I am not attracted to women but damn. She had cunnilingus skills better than any man I know. It had me fucked up for a minute because I didn't stop her when I realized it was her. I continued to let her tongue fuck me to an orgasm. After I came, I put my clothes on and left the hotel. I haven't spoken to her since that day. She would call, but I refused to answer any of her phone calls."

"I don't blame you," Natasha said, obviously as shocked as I was.

"Yeah so that's why, although the ménage started out very exciting, it's hard to tell the story without mentioning that I let a female eat my pussy."

"Well you didn't initially know it was her."

"Yeah but I didn't stop her either when I realized it was her."

"So Natasha, do you have any interesting sex stories," Dianne asked smirking.

"Nope, no story that will top that," Natasha replied still looking shocked.

For a brief moment, we forgot the drama that was currently plaguing our lives. We were able to laugh and have a good time. I don't know where I would be without my best friends.

# Chapter 11

# Aisha's Diary

**WHEN I ARRIVED HOME** after leaving Lynda's house, I couldn't stop thinking about what she told Dianne and me. Tyrone was sound asleep, so to get my mind off Lynda's story, I decided to browse through Aisha's diary that was in the box next to my bed. I didn't want to read Aisha's private thoughts but I can't lie, I was curious as to what she was writing about. I never kept a diary. I flipped around to random pages until something in particular caught my eye.

*Dear Diary,*
*Jason and I just started being girlfriend and boyfriend today. He gave me a friendship ring. My mother told me I could keep it as long as I talked to her first before I let him touch me. I guess she knows what a friendship ring means.*

I smiled to myself and read the next diary entry.

*Dear Diary,*
*Today at Jason's house, something interesting happened. We were playing his Playstation 2 and then he put the game on pause. I wasn't sure what was wrong but he told me he wanted to do something else. I was nervous because he had moved closer to me so I knew he wanted to kiss me or something. He asked if he could touch my breasts. I didn't want to say no so I let him put his hand up my shirt. He lifted my shirt and bra and rubbed my breast. I knew he was nervous because his hands were shaking. He then asked if he could suck on them. I was so scared but, again, I didn't want to say no. He is my boyfriend so I said yes. Jason sucked on my breast so gently and it felt so good. Jason got a hard-on so he asked me to caress his penis. I did. He moaned until his semen was in my hand. I wasn't sure what we were doing but he said it felt good, really good. I was just happy that I could make him feel good.*

I couldn't believe my eyes, but I couldn't stop reading either. Her diary entries were not dated so I couldn't tell when any of this actually happened. My first thought was to be upset, but I have to keep reminding myself that I was sixteen years old myself when I started having sex. *Please don't let me read that she had sex and didn't tell me,* I thought to myself as I continued reading.

*Dear Diary,*
*Today Jason wanted to feel me in my "private place" so I let him. He rubbed it until I felt my panties get wet. I need to talk*

*to my mother because I'm not sure what else Jason is going to want to do next and I have a hard time telling him no. I promised my mother that I wouldn't have sex without talking to her first. I told her today that I was curious about sex, but she didn't look like she was comfortable having the conversation with me yet. I really like Jason and I think I want him to do it to me. He makes me feel good. Maybe I will try talking to her again before Jason wants to touch me again.*

I continued reading in disbelief.

*Dear Diary,*
*I thought I was going to be able to talk to my mother again before Jason and I had sex, but it didn't happen that way.*

I stopped reading for a moment and the tears began to fall. *I think I am about to read how my daughter lost her virginity,* I thought to myself as I tried to get myself together to finish reading the diary entry. I wish I appeared to be more open to the conversation of sex so she would have told me, even if it were after the fact. I continued reading.

*Jason asked me if I could come to his house after school and help him with a project. Of course, I didn't mind helping him because he wasn't just my boyfriend; we had been friends since we were in junior high school. When we got into his room, we began working on his project. After about thirty minutes, he asked if I wanted to take a break. I told him that it didn't matter and he went to get us something to drink. He brought back two sodas. He opened mine first and handed it to me. He was so sweet so I gave him a kiss on the check. That must have excited him because he kissed me on the lips. He asked me to lie back on the bed. When I did, he got on top of me and started grinding on me. After humping me for about ten minutes, he asked if I wanted to do it for real. Of course, I did but I hadn't talked to my mother first. As he unbuttoned my pants, I couldn't stop him. When we were both undressed, he got back on top of me and put his penis inside of me. I wanted to use a condom but Jason said that since neither one of us had sex before, we didn't have a disease. I wasn't considering getting pregnant at that moment. It didn't hurt the way some girls said it did the first time; maybe because he was going slow. I love Jason but I hope I don't get pregnant.*

Pregnant? Is that what I read? I felt the pain of an instant headache and nauseated. Oh no…could my baby have been pregnant and I didn't know it? I started to cry. I wasn't sure what I was about to read in the next diary entry but, I figured, why stop now.

*Dear Diary,*
*I'm scared. I missed my period this month and I don't know what to do. I think I might be pregnant. I am so ashamed to tell my mother because she warned me about not having protected sex and not being on birth control. She was going to take me to the doctor for birth control pills but I didn't think I would be having sex so soon. I should have been more careful. I told Jason that my period is late and he said that whatever happens he would be there for me, but we are so young and I'm scared to have a baby. My mother had me when she was young and I think*

*she regrets it. I always try to be a good child so she won't hate me for being born. I know it's been hard for her to raise me alone because some nights I can hear her crying. I don't want to upset my mother because I know she wants me to go to college and not become a mother at a young age. She always tells me that she wants me to experience the things that she wasn't able to. I would rather die than tell my mother I might be pregnant.*

At that moment, my eyes began to burn so I closed Aisha's diary and closed my eyes. I am so glad that Tyrone is still asleep because I don't plan to share this information with him. It would really hurt him and he is already feeling guilty for not being there for her. I didn't plan on reading anymore of Aisha's diary because what I read already was too painful for me. The words *I would rather die than tell my mother I might be pregnant* kept appearing in my head. Aisha knew that she could always come to me no matter how bad she thought her situation was. I couldn't believe that she would have rather died than come to me. I decided to burn her diary the next chance I could because I didn't want to be tempted to read anymore. Losing my daughter had become more painful.

## Chapter 12

# Motherhood

**THE NEWS OF NELSON BEING A FATHER** was becoming too much for me so I decided to take a vacation alone. I needed some time to think things through. I know Nelson thinks I am considering leaving him, but I am not. I really have to think about how to accept this situation of being a stepmother. Maybe it's time for me to consider having a child of my own. I will be thirty-five next year so maybe it is time to be a mother.

The thought of not being with my husband is too painful, so a divorce is not even in my mind. I think we need time apart to get a grip on how this is going to affect our marriage. It was strange being on vacation without either my husband or my best friends but I wanted to be able to think clearly about what I was feeling. I made sure I spoke to Nelson every morning and every night while I was on vacation. I wanted him to be reassured that I had no intentions on leaving him. I would end every phone conversation at night with "baby I love you and trust that we'll get through this together. I'll see you soon." It was necessary for me to say this not for only Nelson's reassurance but for my own as well.

While I was in Jamaica, there was no "Stella-stuff" going on. I barely left the hotel room. I needed some time to myself. On the morning I was checking out of the hotel, I called Nelson so he would know what time I was due to arrive at Reagan National Airport. He seemed so happy that I was coming home. It was like talking to a kid awaiting the arrival of Santa Claus. I told him we needed to talk when I get home, but I was going into the office for a while. It was Monday morning and I knew he would be at work, and since I would arrive at the office around lunchtime, he offered to bring me lunch so we could talk over lunch. I assured him again that this conversation had nothing to do with me leaving him because that wasn't about to happen. I loved him too much and I really can't imagine my life without him. I do know one thing; I was sure 'nuff horny.

When I arrived at the office, my assistant Pamela was staring at me. I knew it was because she had never seen me without any business attire. I was wearing a gray tennis skirt, a black and gray tank top and a pair of flip-flops. My hair was in a ponytail, which wasn't unusual.

"Good morning, Mrs. Thompson."

"Good morning, *Ms. Woods*," I replied sarcastically because she knows I would rather her call me Dianne.

"Oh, I'm sorry. Good morning, Dianne."

"Thank you. How are you, Pamela?"

"I'm great, how was your vacation?"

"It was very relaxing."

"I put all of your important mail on your desk and the junk mail is in the file folder marked, *Get to it when I can*. The folders for all of the clients you are seeing tomorrow are on your desk in your inbox. Oh yeah, and don't forget about your speaking engagement at the Junior High School on Thursday."

"Thanks, you're great. And here are a couple of souvenirs for you from Jamaica. I know you like collecting key chains and magnets so I bought you a few."

"Wow, thanks for thinking of me, Mrs. Thompson, I mean Dianne. I really appreciate it. But next time could you bring me back a Winston?"

"I don't think that is a good idea," I said, laughing. "We're going to leave all the Winston's in the world right in Jamaica."

Pamela was a young mother who I mentored a few years ago. She was a teenage mother whose parents put her out when they found out she was pregnant. Even though she was living in a shelter, she went to school everyday and graduated from high school on time. Her son was born two weeks after graduation. I think her son remained in the womb so his mama could walk across the stage, receive her diploma and prove everyone wrong. Most people were adamant that she would drop out. I don't understand why people are so negative. Pamela wasn't comfortable going to school pregnant but I encouraged her to remain strong and not let anyone stand in the way of her education. I was so proud of her. Her son's father has been in and out of jail but was recently released, and is working hard to stay out of trouble. Sometimes, good kids are caught up with the wrong kind of things. His crimes were misdemeanors but I'm glad he decided to turn his life around before his crimes turned to felonies.

I paid Pamela more than the job required. I wanted her to be able to support her son with or without help from her son's father, although he did his share. There were times when I told her to bring her son to work when her babysitter was sick or had family emergencies. He was a good little boy so I didn't mind.

Pamela was pretty much my child because I made sure her and her son had whatever they needed. I helped her get her first apartment and I refused to allow her to settle for Section 8 housing. Her parents should have been there for her because she was a great child. Being pregnant doesn't make you a bad person even if you are only sixteen years old. It was always my mission to help at least one child stay off the street. I was determined to make sure she succeeded so I agreed to pay for her college degree through the tuition reimbursement program. She didn't have to pay it upfront and then wait to be reimbursed like many private companies. I paid her tuition for her whenever she wanted to take a class. I felt I should give back because my jobs in the federal government contributed significantly to my education.

It was about 12:30 p.m. when Pamela buzzed me to let me know Nelson had arrived with my lunch. I was so happy to see my husband. Nelson was so thoughtful because he brought lunch for Pamela also. When he walked into my office, I sprang up from my desk and gave him the longest kiss I could remember ever having. He was wearing one of my favorite suits and looking good as always.

"Hi, baby, I missed you," I said, holding on to him.

"I missed you too, sweetheart. How was your trip?"

"It was very relaxing, baby, but I am so glad to be back at home."

*When I'm Loving You*

Nelson brought me Chinese food, which he knows is one of my favorite kinds of food. He was always on point with whatever he selected for me. He bought chicken lo mein and general tsao's chicken. When we were done eating, we sat on the sofa in my office. Normally the sofa is for my clients so it was funny being on it, myself, although Nelson and I have made love on it a few times. Nelson rubbed my thighs while we talked.

"Did you use your vibrator while you were gone?"

"Excuse me?" I said, blushing with embarrassment.

"Yeah I realized it was missing when I was cleaning up. The box is empty. Did you use it?"

"Why Nelson?"

"I'm wondering. I didn't think you used it without me."

Nelson loved watching me with the vibrator. He said that he gets to see me squirm which is impossible to see when he is on top of me. I let him put it in me sometimes, but he said he didn't want to put it in too far and hurt me so he was kind of nervous with it.

"No baby, I didn't use it, but I did take it in case."

"So you must be horny," he said, smiling that same smile he used to get me to sleep with him the first day we met.

As Nelson put his hand up my skirt and rubbed my thighs, he kissed me on my neck. I loved when he kissed my neck. He had a way of allowing his thumb to graze my clit while he caressed my thighs. He knows that drives me wild. It was sort of a teasing move for him. He laid me back on the sofa and pulled down my thongs. He pulled up my skirt and spread my legs apart. He started mumbling so I sat up a little to see what he was saying. He was kissing my pussy and talking to it. He is crazy. He was saying stuff like, 'yes daddy missed you' and 'I couldn't wait to see you.' All I could do was laugh.

While he was reuniting with my pussy, and caressing my thighs, he noticed that my birth control patch was missing.

"Dianne, did your patch come off?"

"No, Nelson. I took it off. That's what I wanted to talk with you about."

"I'm listening."

"I think I'm ready to have a baby."

Nelson sat there and looked at me. I wish I could have read his mind. I know this is too much for him to consider right now because Nelson was already a father and he wasn't sure how that was going to change his life. I could tell he was deep in thought so I continued talking.

"Nelson, you know I love my career but I do want us to have a family. Baby I love you and I love having you to myself but we both know that things are going to change for us now. Nihya is going to want to get to know her biological father even if not right away. I know we can financially support a family so I am not worried about that. I just think that we should start a family together."

Nelson stood up and walked towards the door. My heart dropped and I began to silently cry. Nelson locked the door and walked back over to me. He stood over me as I lay on the sofa. He unzipped his pants and allowed them to drop down around his ankles. When he noticed I was crying, he sat on the edge of the sofa and kissed my tears.

"Baby, why are you crying? What's wrong?" Nelson asked obviously concerned.

"I'm not sure, Nelson. I am so overwhelmed with all this talk about babies and children."

"Well you said you wanted us to have a family right?"

"Yes, but–"

"But what? You want us to have a family so let's start now."

Nelson took off the rest of his clothes and climbed on top of me. His power tool was so hard. I couldn't wait for him to be inside of me. As he made love to me in my office, the passion was different some how. He looked me in my eyes as he penetrated me. I was still crying but they were tears of joy. He continued to kiss my tears as they fell. I think I even saw a tear fall down his cheek.

༄ ༄ ༄ ༄ ༄

After Nelson and I climaxed together, he began rubbing my stomach. "One day, I'll be rubbing your stomach with our child growing inside of you."

I was so emotional that I couldn't even speak. I looked into his eyes and continued to cry.

"Do you know how long you have to be off the patch to be able to conceive?" Nelson asked me still rubbing my stomach. It appeared that he was excited about being a father.

"I'm not sure. I'll call my OB/GYN to ask him tomorrow."

At that moment, I thought about the miscarriage that I had in my early twenties. The pain of not carrying my baby to term was too much for me and that was one of the reasons I wasn't in a rush to start a family. Could I even carry a baby to term? I wasn't sure and I didn't want to disappoint Nelson with a failed pregnancy. I had never shared that with Nelson and I was wondering how he would accept the news of our child not being my first pregnancy. I had a way of blocking out painful memories from my past. Specializing in Psychology, I knew that could lead to very destructive behaviors. I was beginning to think maybe I should seek counseling myself to make sure I haven't suppressed any other painful memories.

## Chapter 13

# The Book Signing

**IT WOULD BE MONTHS** before I would see Zion again. His book was finished and he was having a book signing. I was happy for him although I was still hurting that I didn't really have a chance to get to know him. I still decided to support his book and go to his book signing. When it was my turn to get my copy of his book signed, he must have only written his name because he sure did autograph it very quickly. I was hurting so bad that I didn't even look at him. As I walked away, the tears started to fall. I hurried to the nearest restroom so I could cry. I really couldn't believe that after all this time, I was still crying over Zion. I felt a connection with him that I simply could not explain and I was completely drained trying to figure it all out.

When I finally gained the nerve to read what Zion wrote in the book, I turned to the first page and it was a poem entitled,

# K. Lowery Moore

*My Soul Mate.* Above the poem, he wrote, *For Lynda, Love Zion.* The poem read:

> We communicate to each other without saying a word
> Your thoughts speak to me
> When words are not heard
> Though this may sound absurd to some,
> Others know exactly what I mean
> Whenever I'm near you, it's like I'm living in a dream
> And I don't want to wake up
> From the moment I sat down next to you
> I felt something between us
> I've learned to trust my instincts
> Because they are more than just...gut feelings
> Even if we don't act on our feelings
> It's no question the chemistry is there
> But not acting on our feelings
> The question is, 'would that be fair?'
> I've tried to play it off, but I can't hide it
> Not to think about you, baby I've tried it
> And believe me, it's not easy dealing with this situation
> I really don't need this complication
> Because I love you,
> And you don't know if you want to be with him
> But if we aren't honest with ourselves,
> Does anyone really win?
> When I'm alone, I would rather you be there
> You say he's there for you, but I really don't care
> Can't you see, my soul speaks to your soul
> And you can't get a deeper connection

## When I'm Loving You

*This is more than simple affection*
*And please don't say it; it's not even about sex*
*You know that's not the mission, that's not what this is*
*It's much deeper than that and as a matter of fact*
*My feelings for you have reached a depth*
*Until now unknown*
*Although we've spent some time apart,*
*My love for you have grown*
*And it's not okay that you are considering him*
*Understand I'm not pressuring you*
*But we also cannot pretend*
*It's very real, how we both feel*
*So let's enjoy this like our favorite dance*
*But think about it, nothing we do is simply by chance*
*We are where we are for a reason*
*And in each season, God knows what He is doing*
*But most of the time we fail to listen*
*So ask yourself, what am I missing?*
*The answer may very well be your soul mate.*

After reading Zion's poem, I washed my face, touched up my makeup and left the restroom. Zion was waiting for me outside of the restroom. When I walked out, he wrapped me in his arms. He kissed me on my cheek and whispered in my ear, "I was hoping that you would come. We need to talk." Normally I would be evasive when someone says that they need to talk, but somehow this sounded like good news. The way he was holding me, I knew it had to be good news.

The book signing wasn't over so Zion asked if we could meet for dinner later that evening. Of course, I agreed although

I wasn't sure if what Zion wanted to talk about was going to be favorable or not. I needed to be strong and hear him out because, either way, I was in love with him and, if nothing else, I wanted us to be at least friends.

I made sure I looked extra special for my dinner date with Zion. The weather was beautiful so I put on my black spaghetti strap sundress and my black strappy stiletto sandals. I made sure I had a fresh French pedicure because Zion loved pretty feet. When he arrived at house, he rang the doorbell; I opened the door to two-dozen white roses. I loved white roses, but I don't remember telling him that. I'm sure he picked up on that in one of our many conversations. I love men who pay attention to small details. Zion must have liked what he saw because his manhood instantly rose. *Damn it's like that*, I thought to myself as I gave him a hug.

"Girl, I've missed you so much. I can't even express how much."

"I think you can express it," I said, smiling as I pointed to his erection. "I've missed you too, Zion. Thank you so much for the roses. White roses are my favorite."

Zion gave me one of those wet, but not too sloppy, kisses he was famous for. He caressed my ass and pulled me closer to him. I guess he wanted me to feel how happy he was to see me. I wanted him to make love to me right then and there but I was looking way too cute for us not to go on our date.

"Let me put these flowers in some water and I will be ready to go."

"Girl, you look so good."

"Thanks, I wanted to look good for you."

"Well, I'm glad because you look and smell amazing. But we do need to talk to clear up some things."

Damn, Zion always made me nervous whenever he said we needed to talk. "Should we stay here and talk?"

"No, I have dinner reservations. Oh yeah, sorry for the last minute but can you stay the night with me?"

"Sure. I don't have anything pressing to do tomorrow."

"Okay, cool. Go pack a few things, especially some comfortable clothes. Do you have some cute shorts? I would love to see you in a pair. Not with your ass out though. I want us to spend the day at the Baltimore Harbor tomorrow."

"Yes Zion, I think I can find a pair of cute shorts, without my ass being out," I answered sarcastically.

He laughed. I went upstairs and packed an overnight bag. I found lingerie I had bought that still had the tag on it. I made sure I packed my black lace stilettos. He was in for a treat tonight. This must not be bad news if he wants me to spend the weekend with him. But who knows. This might be the set up for the let down. Again, I need to think positive. I don't think he would be going through all of this to tell me we couldn't be together. Then again, I don't know.

I prayed for a man to sweep me off my feet and Zion was doing that. He does the things that I like for a man to do without me having to ask. With Zion, I felt like I could be the woman that I want to be. I could be that delicate flower knowing that I would be handled with care. I messed up with Zion but I think God is giving me another chance. I am a firm believer that if something was meant to be, it'll be.

Zion took me to Ruth's Chris Steak House, near the Baltimore Inner Harbor, for dinner and we had such a great time. I couldn't wait until our day tomorrow at the Baltimore Harbor. After dinner, we went to a nearby hotel. I was so ecstatic to finally be with Zion again. When we settled into our room, Zion ran a bath for us. There were candles all around the bathroom; so many of them, I was worried the room was going to catch on fire. When did he have time to set all this up? How did he even know that I would say yes and stay the night with him? The tub was a nice big Jacuzzi style tub. Bubbles in the tub, petals of red roses were sprinkled on the floor and incense and scented candles gave the perfect ambience for a night to remember. It was so romantic. I was horny too. It had been a while since I had seen Zion or Taye so I wasn't having sex with anyone at the time. I was well overdue for an orgasm, then again multiple orgasms.

The passion between us was so intense in the tub. We kissed and caressed each other as if it was our first time together, even though it had been several months since our last encounter. I really missed him and from what I can tell, he missed me too.

"You know I want you right here."

"Zion," I said, looking around the bathroom, "you know you don't have protection in here."

"I know, but I want you so bad. I miss being inside of you."

"Well let's get out of the tub."

We didn't get a chance to make use of the lingerie and black lace stilettos that I brought with me. I'm sure there will be another opportunity for me to put them on for him. He laid me on the bed and kissed me all over. Then he stopped and asked me, "When was the last time you had sex Lynda?"

"Zion, why are you asking me that now?" I asked him because I was really confused.

"I'm curious."

"Well probably about two months or so. Why?"

"During those two months, what did you do when you got horny or did you get horny?"

"I would try to think about something else and if that didn't work then I would take matters into my own hands."

"Is that right?" he responded sounding excited.

"Yes, that is right."

"You mean you masturbate?"

"Yeah Zion," I said, annoyed. "Are you going to put it in or what?"

"Naw, I want you to show me what you do when you are alone."

"Huh?"

"Masturbate for me."

"No, Zion, come on!" I said, caressing the head of his penis.

"Please," he said, as he took my hand and placed it between my legs, "that is a turn on for me."

I wasn't comfortable at first with what Zion was asking me to do. Being alone is one thing, but to do it in front of a man was something totally different.

"Zion, that is personal."

"Let me get you started."

Zion took my hand and sucked on my middle finger. He then took that finger and pushed it inside of me. He sucked on my breasts to get me more aroused. It was working. I moved my finger in and out of me as he talked dirty in my ear. I was so turned on by what he was asking me to do. I guess he couldn't take the demonstration anymore because he put on a condom, moved my hand and entered me with such passion. Zion was making love to me and reciting poetry in my ear, in French! It was simply incredible. I don't know what he was actually saying because I took Spanish and not French. However, it didn't even matter what he was saying to me at that time because his sexy voice was turning me on. That may have been the best sex I ever had or at least based on what I could remember. I mean it was so good that I don't remember falling asleep. I remember having an orgasm so intense that it made my legs tremble ferociously for several minutes.

When I woke up the next morning, Zion had already taken the liberty to order room service. He knew exactly what to order because he pays attention to the things I like and don't like. That is a great quality that more men should possess. After we ate breakfast, we headed for the shower. We took turns washing each other. It was so refreshing being there with Zion. After the shower, I dressed in my cute shorts, without my ass hanging out, that Zion had requested and a halter-top. He smiled a smile of approval and nodded his head as if to say, "*I like that!*"

Our day together at the Baltimore Harbor was simply beautiful. We went to the aquarium and then paddle boating. After that, it was time for lunch at the Cheesecake Factory at the harbor. Zion wanted to play a few games at the ESPN Zone but I was tired so instead we went to the nearest movie theatre. We sat close during the movie and enjoyed each other. Occasionally Zion would caress my thighs but I told him that he had to stop because it was turning me on. I hadn't been on a date like this in years, where my date and I spent the entire day together. I really liked the courting stage of a romantic relationship.

*When I'm Loving You*

I did not want the day to end, but of course, it would have to end at some point. "Zion, what are you doing tonight after you take me home?"

"I was hoping you would let me spend the night with you. Or is that too much for one weekend?"

"I would love for you to stay with me tonight."

"Well, that's what's up."

When we returned to my place, I was so exhausted. I didn't even feel like taking shower, but I did anyway. I could tell Zion was tired too because we both finished our shower in record time. Before I went to sleep, I had a few important questions to ask him.

"Zion, how do you feel about me?"

"I'm really feeling you, Lynda, and I am hoping this is the beginning of us getting to know each other as more than friends."

"I do too." Satisfied with his response, I lay in his arms until I drifted off to sleep.

At some point in the middle of the night, Zion must have gotten horny because I woke up with his hand between my legs. "I thought that would wake you up. You still tired?"

"I was sleeping, Zion, but if you want me, baby, I'm right here."

"You sure because I will let you sleep if you want."

"No, I'm up now."

Before Zion penetrated me, he whispered in my ear, "I um, I love you, Lynda, and I hope you love me."

His words penetrated me deeply. I inhaled and whispered back, "Aw Zion, yes I love you," and before I knew it, I was crying. It's been a long time since I felt safe in the arms of a man.

"Baby, is something bothering you. Do you want to talk?"

Here we go with the talking again. "No, I'm okay. I'm happy that's all. It's been a while since I felt like I could let my guard down. You allow me to be the woman I desire to be and that is so important to me. I'm afraid though; relationships are hard for me. I haven't been in a committed relationship in a long time and I'm scared."

"Baby don't be scared, I know that's easy for me to say but I love you and I want you to be my girl. Those few months away from you was torture for me. I should have been more understanding of what you were going through, but I don't think I would have been able to handle it if you would have chosen him over me. To show you that I was serious about starting a relationship with you, I decided to put the poem I wrote for you in my book. You know the one I recited for you the night I took you to the poetry reading. Although I had to change it up a bit." Finally, I knew what Zion was saying that night on the stage.

"What if I hadn't come to your book signing?"

"I would have come to find you, but somehow I had faith that you would be there. I don't know why but I felt it."

As I am lying beside Zion, I thought of a short poem and I whispered in his ear. I've been writing more poetry since I met Zion, although I needed to be completing my novel.

*All I need is to be held and gently caressed*
*Kissed all over and slowly undressed*
*Handled with care by my Nubian brotha*
*Soulfully unite as we embrace one another*
*The feel of your flesh against my naked skin*
*The warmth of my body wants to welcome you in*

### *When I'm Loving You*

*But right now, all I need is for you to hold me*
*Tightly in your arms because I've been so lonely*

Zion held me in his arms and passionately kissed me. He didn't pressure me to have sex although I knew he wanted to because he still had a serious erection. Again, I fell asleep in his arms. I'm sure I've said this before but I prayed for a man to sweep me off my feet and Zion was doing a very good job of it. I was still scared to totally let go of my feelings because I wasn't sure how long this was going to last. I need to learn from Dianne, because she always says that there are no guarantees in life so we need to enjoy whatever we have, for however long we have it.

## CHAPTER 14

# Ex–Wife

**FOR THE PAST YEAR OR SO**, my menstrual cycle has not been regular, according to my doctor it was due to stress. Therefore, the fact that missing a few periods might mean I was pregnant did not register in my mind right away. It wasn't until the morning sickness began that I realized I might be pregnant so I went to the OB/GYN for a pregnancy test. I decided to get a pap smear also because obviously Tyrone and I hadn't been using condoms every time we had sex. My Pap smear results were normal and my pregnancy test was positive. According to the doctor, I was about eight weeks pregnant.

I wasn't sure if having Tyrone's baby was a good idea because we weren't married and I didn't want to make the same mistake twice. I do love him but I am not sure if he is the right man for me. However, I need him in my life right now. When I told Tyrone I was pregnant, he seemed very happy. He hadn't been divorced long so I was worried that maybe we were moving too fast. He assured me his marriage was over long before it was actually over and he never stopped loving me. He explained why Annie came up here to Maryland ready to fight me; he talked about me all the time. I've always known he wasn't in love with the woman he married but the fact was he still married someone else to get back at me for leaving.

I guess the news of me being pregnant with Tyrone's baby has really pissed of his ex-wife Annie so she was determined to make things rough for him. He still had some things at their house he had to pick up. Their house was under contract by a potential buyer and the settlement date was less than a month away. I don't know why Tyrone told Annie I was pregnant, but it sparked some serious unnecessary drama.

Tyrone and I flew to Georgia so he could get the rest of his things out of the house. We stayed at a hotel in Atlanta. I went with him so I could see some of the few friends I did have in Georgia, before I moved, since I didn't make it to my ten-year class reunion. Tyrone was planning to rent a U-Haul truck to move his stuff to my condo, but I was catching a flight back to Washington, DC. The drive from Georgia is too much for me right now since I am going into the second trimester stage of my pregnancy. I wasn't sure if being in Georgia was going to be a good idea for me in case Annie broke lose and wanted to fight me. I was in no condition to fight anyone. Tyrone was confident that nothing out of the ordinary was going to happen and that Annie was over him. I don't know why men don't see what women see. I could see the drama coming because she wanted to have a baby while they were married and he kept putting it off by always saying that maybe the following year would be a better time. Well of course that time never came and now I was carrying the baby she wanted to carry.

I suggested to Tyrone that he get a police escort while he removed belongings from the house. Of course, he thought I was overreacting and that getting a police escort was too extreme. I pleaded with him not to put anything past a woman scorned.

"Tyrone, anytime a female travels all those miles to fight someone that she feels destroyed her marriage; it's no telling what else she is capable of doing."

"I don't think a police escort is necessary, I ain't no punk."

"It's not about you being a punk Tyrone, but I can't force you to take the necessary precautions so be careful. I don't want to have to say I told you so."

"Come on Natasha, nothing is going to happen. I don't have much still in there anyway. It's just my clothes, shoes and stuff like that. Other than that, I just want my big screen TV. She can have all that other furniture."

"Alright Tyrone, call me on my cell later on."

I kissed him and he left the hotel room. I hope Tyrone is right that Annie wouldn't give him any drama. I am not in the mood for any nonsense. I am ready for Tyrone and me to move on with our lives.

※ ※ ※ ※ ※

I had a great time with my friends in Atlanta, but I hadn't heard from Tyrone in about four hours. He should have been finished by now so I began to worry. My flight was scheduled to leave in the morning and I wanted to spend some time with

Tyrone before I left. I called his cell phone several times but I didn't get an answer. I noticed that I had a message on my cell phone so I checked it, in case it was Tyrone, but it was from Dianne. Her message said, "Hey Natasha this is Dianne call me as soon as you get this message, it's really important. It's about Tyrone." I stood there for a moment and stared at nothing in particular.

When I returned Dianne's call, she answered on the first ring. "Natasha, what took you so long to call me back, Tyrone is in trouble."

"What? How do you know that?" I asked with teary eyes.

"I guess he couldn't call you collect on your cell phone so he called me and Lynda. Lynda and I weren't home but he was able to reach Nelson and Nelson called me."

"He's not hurt is he Dianne, please tell me he is not hurt. I can't handle this right now."

"I know calm down. We didn't want to upset you but Tyrone is in jail and he needs you to contact his lawyer right away. He also told Nelson to tell you that you were right and he should have listened to you. What did you tell him?"

"Oh shit, something must have happened with Annie when he went to get his stuff from the house. I told him to call for a police escort as a precaution. She is not wrapped too tight."

"Girl, apparently she is saying that Tyrone assaulted her."

"What? Well okay, give me his lawyer's information. This is so stupid. Some women can be so damn immature. It's ridiculous. It's over so move on, damn!"

"I know Natasha, but don't you upset yourself. You don't just have yourself to worry about right now. It's all going to work out."

*When I'm Loving You*

"I really hope so. I don't need this right now. I really don't."

"Well call me after you talk with the lawyer," Dianne said, before she hung up.

"This is what the fuck I was talking about," I said out loud. "Why couldn't Tyrone listen to me? I know a woman's mind."

When I contacted the lawyer, he said he had spoken with Tyrone briefly about the situation and that I needed to meet with him first thing Monday morning.

"Monday? I'm supposed to fly back to DC tomorrow. But I guess I have to change my flight. I don't need this."

"I know Ms. Inglewood, Tyrone mentioned you were pregnant. You might not remember me, but Tyrone and I were friends right after high school. We weren't friends in school because they use to call me a nerd and said that I was going to get jumped being so nerdy. When I told Tyrone that I was going to college to be a lawyer, he was encouraged to go to college for accounting. He said he wanted his mother to be proud of him."

"Oh yeah, you were the nice boy his mother always spoke so highly of all the time. Ma Price used to say when Tyrone started running the streets, 'why can't Tyrone be more like that Jonathan boy.' He really hated when his mother would compare him to you."

"Yeah, I was that Jonathan boy his mother was referring to," he said, laughing. "I'm glad that you and Tyrone are back together. He never stopped loving you. Don't tell him I told you, but the day you left Georgia, he cried like a punk ass. We were on the basketball court shooting hoops and one of the guys asked how you were doing. He just broke down and cried

141

in front of all his boys. That's how we knew he loved you. To this day, I still haven't cried over a woman so you must be really special."

"I guess I am," I said, laughing and he laughed with me.

"The fellas tried to warn him not to marry Annie because we all knew he was just on the rebound. But after losing his mother and losing you, he felt getting married would be the best way for him to try to move on with his life."

"I kind of figured that. But, what could I do? I had to think about Aisha and she was my priority."

"I know and trust me; Tyrone highly respects your decision because he realizes he messed up by hanging with the wrong crowd back then."

"Yeah but I am a firm believer that all of this has happened for a reason."

"Yeah, that is true. Well, I'll see you Monday at the courthouse. We are going to get through this so don't worry. Tyrone is my boy and I told him I would always be there for his punk ass," he laughed, again.

Hearing Jonathan's story of the basketball court made me love Tyrone even more. What man do you know is going to cry in front of his boys over a female?

What was I going to do in Atlanta by myself tomorrow? I called Dianne to let her know that I had spoken with Tyrone's lawyer.

"Hey Dianne," I said, trying to hold back my tears.

"Hey girl, did you talk to the lawyer?"

"Yes and we're going to get him out of jail on Monday." *That's the only thing about getting locked up on the weekend. You have to wait until Monday and Lord help you if that*

## When I'm Loving You

*Monday is a holiday.* I thought to myself before I said goodbye to Dianne.

On Monday, I met with Jonathan so we could bail Tyrone out of jail. When he walked into the receiving area, he shook Jonathan's hand while he held me with one arm. He whispered in my ear, "Baby, I'm sorry I didn't listen to you. All of this could have been avoided if I had just listened to you. And don't say it because yeah you told me so."

I smiled and kissed him on the cheek. We left the court building and went to Jonathan's office so Tyrone could tell his side of the story.

"When I got to the house to get the rest of my stuff, a lot of my things had been destroyed. However, I decided not to worry about it because it was all material stuff and could be bought again. So as I gathered what had not been either cut up or burned, she walks up to me with a see-through nightgown talking about she wanted to show me one last time what I would be missing. She became furious when I didn't pay her any attention and starting throwing stuff at me. So, I figured I just leave with whatever I had already packed and then do what Natasha suggested in the first place. As I walked out of the door, she jumped on my back, I guess to stop me from leaving. She kept screaming, 'fuck me one last time, please Tyrone, fuck me one last time.' I was so disgusted that I shook her off my back. She hit the floor kind of hard and then she called the police and said that I body slammed her on the floor, after trying to force her to have sex. I couldn't believe it. Before I could get my stuff in the U-Haul, the police was there ready to arrest my black ass."

I sat there, shaking my head, with tears running down my cheeks. Tyrone looked at me with a painful look in his eyes.

**143**

"I'm so sorry Natasha baby, to put you through this nonsense. Please forgive me."

"There is nothing to forgive, Tyrone. You did what you thought was best considering you were married to her. I know you were hoping that all would be well and you could move on peacefully. It doesn't happen like that with most women. Just be glad you don't have any children with her because your life would be a living hell as long as you lived. Women can be very vindictive."

"Well, I mean you weren't like that Tash when we split up," Tyrone said, as if all women are supposed to be alike.

"That's because, although I love you, I love myself more."

Jonathan looked up from his note pad and nodded in my direction as if to say *good answer*.

As Tyrone's court date grew near, he became more concerned about the outcome of the case. I was close to six months pregnant and Tyrone felt he had let me down, again. I loved Tyrone, so I was willing to stand by his side. Every evening, when he would get home from work, I would give him a massage to help him relax. He would then rub my stomach and back and also massage my legs and feet like when I was pregnant with Aisha. He had no problem with the pregnant pussy either.

The day before the court date, we flew to Georgia. I encouraged Tyrone to get some rest because he hadn't been sleeping much since the incident with Annie, who I like to call, Crazy. As we lay in the bed in the hotel room, Tyrone kissed my stomach and spoke to our baby, which the doctor said was a boy. When he would talk, the baby kicked. He kicked hard too. "That's my man, a future NFL punter," Tyrone said, grinning from ear to ear.

*When I'm Loving You*

"Tyrone, do you want to name our son?" I asked rubbing the back of his head.

"You would let me name him? I remember you cursed me out when I tried to suggest a name for Aisha."

"I was young and not fair to you. Fathers should be involved in naming their child. Now if you come up with something off the wall, then I am going to have to override you," I laughed.

"See what I'm saying?" he laughed. "But yes I would like to name him. How about Tyrin?"

"I like that but I'm surprised you don't want him to be a junior."

"I thought about it, but Tyrin is close to my name."

"What if by chance the doctor is wrong and our baby is a girl?

"Then we can name her Tyra or Tyisha," he smiled, "just as long as it is close to my name."

Before I could respond, Tyrone grabbed my hand and kissed it. He looked me in the eyes and a single tear fell down his cheek. I can tell he was trying to stop it but it was too late.

"Tash, thank you for not giving up on me. You are a good woman and, at times, I feel I don't deserve you. God is giving me another chance to be a good father and another chance to do right by you."

Tyrone gently pulled me up off the bed and led me out onto the balcony. It was a beautiful night. The stars were shining bright, as if they were twinkling for this special moment.

"Natasha baby, I love you so much. I can't imagine my life without you so I was wondering if you will be my wife."

"Tyrone just because I'm pregnant you don't have to—"

Before I could finish my statement, he pulled a small box from his pocket, bent down on one knee, and said, "Natasha Inglewood, will you marry me?"

"Yes Tyrone Price. I will marry you and be your wife," I said, as the tears fell from my eyes.

Tyrone put the ring on my finger and led me back into the bedroom. He was extra gentle with me when we made love since I was pregnant. I found it more comfortable to let him enter me from behind while I lay on my right side. Of course, he didn't mind because my ass was huge. He loved me in this position because he could penetrate me from the back while caressing my breasts that grew from the size of oranges to the size of grapefruits. If we were in the front of a mirror, Tyrone was even more excited.

Court day arrived and Tyrone was nervous. We went inside and sat down beside his lawyer Jonathan, who was already there. I looked around the courtroom and Annie was not there. I was praying she wouldn't come because the charges would be dropped and the case would be thrown out. My prayers were answered. Annie was a no show and the case was dismissed. Now Tyrone and I can go back to Maryland and get on with our lives. At least I hope so!

## Chapter 15

# Painful Story

**NELSON'S EX-GIRLFRIEND MARIE** doesn't have much longer to live. Whenever Hospice comes in to take care of someone, it's not a good sign. Hospice is an organization that makes terminal patients comfortable during their final days. I used to wish my mother hadn't died suddenly, but now I think watching someone die slowly is much harder. Nihya is trying to be so strong, but I can see how it is tearing her up inside that she is losing her mother. She reminds me of myself when I was her age; so determined to stay strong. I know watching Marie die is also hard for Nelson because he was in love with her at one point in his life.

Since it's the summertime, Nihya has been spending a lot of time with Nelson and me. I took a leave of absence for a few weeks to make sure she has something fun to do to help keep her mind of her mother's terminal situation. I really wish I could take all of her pain away, but of course, I cannot. At first it took some time getting use to having someone else in my house full-time, but now I am actually going to miss her when it's time for her to go back to the father who raised her.

Nelson didn't want her to leave, but he wasn't sure if a custody battle was going to be good for Nihya at this moment. I suggested that we all sit down to decide what was going to be best for Nihya. She was most definitely going to need a mother figure in her life.

It was the day before we were going to take Nihya back to her home and Nelson hadn't gotten home yet. I wanted to help her pack all of the clothes that I had bought when we went shopping together.

"Nihya, let me help you pack so you can go home."

"Am I going to my grandma's house?" She asked, almost pleading.

"No, your father wants you to come home."

When I said that, she stood in the middle of the floor and urinated on herself. Something definitely was upsetting this child. As a psychologist, I knew something was wrong. I thought maybe she was scared that her mother was dying.

"Nihya, what's wrong sweetheart?" I asked, trying to stay calm.

That's when she ran over to me and grabbed me around the waist and begged for me not to take her back home. I couldn't understand what was going on with her but the way she was crying, this was something very serious.

"Please don't take me home. I'll be good. I can go to school from here, I make good grades, I know how to wash dishes, and I can help you and my daddy around the house. Just don't take me home to him. Please, no!"

At that moment, I was in tears. "Nihya, what's wrong, does Walter hurt you?"

She nodded without looking at me.

"Nihya, does he hit you?"

She didn't respond. She looked up at me with tears falling down her cheeks. Finally, she said something that would change everything. "He doesn't hit me, but he still hurt me. "

I already knew what that meant, but she needed to tell me herself. I didn't want to feed anything into her mind.

"Nihya, do you want to tell me what he does to you?"

"I'm scared."

"Why Nihya? You are safe here."

"But my mommy is already sick and I don't want to upset her and make her die faster."

"Oh no, Nihya, why would you think that?"

"He said that if I told anyone, it would upset my mommy and make her die faster. I know I am already going to lose her, but I don't want it to be faster than it already is going to be."

"Nihya, trust me. That is not going to happen. I won't take you home; I promise if he is doing things to you to hurt you, you can tell me. "

"He told me that since my mommy was sick in the hospital that he needed me so he wouldn't see other women. At first he only told me to touch him."

"Touch him where?"

"Touch him down his pants. I didn't want to, I swear, but he told me that I had to in order to keep our family together."

"Okay, you said that's all at first. What else did he asked you to do?"

"He then wanted to touch me. At first he used his hands but then, he—" She stopped and began to cry.

"Nihya, we don't have to finish talking now if you don't want to. You want to take a break?"

"No, I think I can tell you. He would take his fingers and put them between my legs at first, but one day he wanted to put his private part inside of me and he did."

I wanted to die at that moment. I never understood how a grown man could do this to a child, not to mention a child he was raising. But unfortunately, being in the field that I am in, I see cases like this more often than I would really like to.

"That's why I don't want to go home because I don't want him to do that to me anymore."

"And he won't."

"Are you going to tell my daddy?"

"Nihya, I have to because he is your father and he wouldn't want anyone to hurt you ever again."

"I don't want him to be upset with me too."

"He's not going to be upset sweetheart, he's going to want to protect you and I am going to help him."

"But I know you going to tell my grandma and the police, right?"

"Nihya, you are going to have to tell the police what you just told me, okay? I can tell your grandma if you want me to."

"Okay. But what about my mother, does she have to know? I don't want to upset her. She is already sick."

*When I'm Loving You*

"Take a shower so you can change your clothes and go to bed. I'll call your father and tell him that we are not bringing you home tonight," I said, avoiding her question.

I really couldn't believe what I had heard. This child is going way too much and she shouldn't have to. Trauma like this follows a person into adulthood and some are strong enough to cope but others are not. I knew I had a long road ahead of me being a stepmother to Nihya. I guess now is not the time for Nelson and I to have baby. We have to help his little girl through the traumatic situation of being sexually abused for who knows how long. Plus her mother is dying. Lord, give me strength to help her through all of this. Now I have to figure out how to break this to Nelson. It's really going to break his heart to know the truth of what's been happening to Nihya.

෴ ෴ ෴ ෴ ෴

When Nelson came home, he had tears in his eyes. I could tell he must have had some bad news about Nihya's mother.

"Nelson baby, talk to me."

"She's gone, Di. Marie died this afternoon."

"Nelson, I'm so sorry."

"I went to see her, to talk to her about Nihya living with us because she is going to need a mother. All she said to me was to please keep our baby girl safe. And that she knows she would be safe with us. Her mom was there too and she is taking it so hard. It was really painful to see her die. Dianne, I don't want to see the pain in Nihya's eyes. I don't think I can handle telling her."

Nelson cried so hard in my arms. I have always known that Marie was his high school sweetheart. He never told me details about their relationship and he never once spoke badly about her whenever he did briefly discuss their relationship. Generally that's how you can tell if a person really loved their former girlfriend or boyfriend because they don't speak negative of them.

"Nelson, I can tell her if you want me to. I can let her know that I lost my mother too when I was a little girl. Although she knew her mother was going to die, of course the reality is going to break her heart. Actually maybe it would be better if we told her together."

"I would like that baby. Thank you for sticking with me through this. You are truly an amazing woman."

"That's because I have an amazing husband," I said, softly kissing Nelson on the lips.

It really hurt me to see Nelson in pain like this. Unfortunately, there is nothing you can do for a person who has suffered a great loss. They have to deal with their pain and be allowed to grieve. At this point, I didn't know how I was going to tell Nelson about Nihya being sexually abused. But I had to figure out a way to tell him. However, there was going to be no easy way and I didn't want him to be upset with me for not telling him right away.

"Nelson, there is something very important that I need to tell you. I was talking to Nihya tonight and she told me that Walter has been molesting her."

"What!"

I could see so many mixed emotions on Nelson's face. He was crying and using words I don't think I have ever heard come from him.

"When I told her we were taking her home in the morning she became so terrified that she urinated on herself. Then she started begging and pleading to stay here with us. Nelson, I don't know what to do. I feel so helpless."

Nelson started pacing the floor. He was in total disbelief. "I wonder if that's why Marie said for me to keep our daughter safe. I wonder if she suspected something. I can't believe he took advantage of Nihya and stole her innocence. I could really kill him right about now."

"Baby, please don't do anything. In the morning, we can report this to the police and let them handle this. Okay Nelson?" Somehow, I knew Nelson wasn't going to listen to me.

I woke up in the middle of the night and Nelson was not in the bed. *Lord, what has he gone to do?* I thought to myself as I instantly became worried. I called his cell phone several times but he didn't answer. I said a silent prayer that Nelson hadn't gone to do anything that would land him in jail. That really would not help the situation.

About two hours later Nelson walked in the house. I was waiting for him in the family room.

"Nelson, where were you?"

"I went for a drive to clear my head."

"Are you sure you went for just a drive?" I asked because I could almost always tell when he wasn't telling me the whole truth.

"Well—"

"Well what Nelson?" I asked, raising my voice.

"Okay, I understand that you are upset but don't raise your voice at me. I'm a grown muthafucking man and I can go and come as the fuck I please."

"Whoa!" That was all I could say because in all the years we have been married, Nelson has never cursed at me. Then all of sudden I became very angry. "Wait a fucking minute. Who do you think you are cursing at Nelson?" The tears began falling down my cheeks. "I'm your wife and not some bitch off the street."

"Well right now I can't tell the difference."

"Did you just call me a bitch?" Now I was furious.

At that moment, I saw a side of Nelson that I didn't know existed. He started throwing and breaking stuff in the family room. I was too scared to stop him. All I could do was plead with him to talk to me but nothing I said calmed him down. It wasn't until Nihya came downstairs crying. All of the commotion must have woken her up.

"Are you fighting because of me?" Nihya asked with a stream of tears falling. "I'm sorry to be such a problem, but please don't fight. I'm sorry that I let him touch me and didn't say no. I should have said no and I'm sorry. I knew better but I was scared to say no. He said that he could hurt me in other ways too if I didn't let him."

Nelson picked her up and held her in his arms. I have never seen him in so much pain. I didn't know what to do to help him.

"He will never come near you again. I promise you that," he told Nihya.

I went upstairs to give him sometime with Nihya. So much was going on that she didn't know yet that her mother was gone.

When Nelson came into our bedroom, he really looked like a broken man.

"Nelson baby talk to me," I said, rubbing his back as he sat on the edge of the bed.

"Dianne, I'm sorry. There is no excuse for me to disrespect you like that. I am so angry, but I should not have taken it out on you. You have been very supportive during this difficult time and I appreciate you so much."

"I understand sweetheart, but I was concerned about you. You didn't go see Walter did you?"

The way he looked at me I knew that he did go. I'm praying that he didn't do anything other than talk to him.

"When I got there, he immediately let me in because he thought something was wrong with Nihya. He just didn't seem concerned that Marie died. I don't know, maybe he was in shock. I didn't beat around the bush. I let him know that Nihya said that he was molesting her. Of course, he denied it and said that she was just upset about losing her mother. That she was making up stories for attention. I asked him why Nihya would need attention when her mother was dying. She didn't know her mother was even dead yet. He didn't say too much other than she was lying. I just let it be known that if it was confirmed that she was being sexually abused that he would definitely regret it."

"Nelson, I understand that you want to take matters into your own hands, but please let the police handle this." I said, as I massage his shoulders hoping that would relax him a little. "

"I will make an appointment for Nihya to get examined to see if there is evidence that she has been penetrated and then we can go to the police with this. She has agreed to tell them what he was doing to her but she doesn't want to go back there."

"And she doesn't have to. I will put up a fight for her. Thank you so much baby. Now we just have to let her know in the morning that her mother is gone."

"I know but let's just try to get some rest. We have a long day ahead of us tomorrow."

~ ~ ~ ~ ~

The next morning, I was cooking breakfast while Nelson was reading the paper. Nihya came downstairs asking if she could go to the hospital to see her mother. Nelson broke down crying, so I had to be strong for the both of them.

"Why is my daddy crying? Did my mommy die already?" Nihya asked with tears in her eyes.

All I could do was nod my head. The pain in her eyes broke my heart.

"But I didn't have a chance to say goodbye to her. Why did she leave me without at least saying goodbye?"

"Nihya, I know this is hard for you but your daddy and I will be here for you. And your grandma is too. I lost my mother too when I was a little girl so I understand how you feel." I couldn't hold the tears any longer. We all sat there and cried.

Death is hard whether it is sudden or expected. Losing a parent at such a young age is especially hard. I never got over the loss of my mother. I grew up feeling abandoned. My stepmother was wonderful but it still didn't fill that void of not having my mother here. With every accomplishment, I wish she could have been here to say how proud she was of me. Hopefully Nihya will continue to be as strong as she is now, but this is going to be a long healing process and I will always be there for her. She is really going to need someone to love her unconditionally and I am going to be one of those people.

## Chapter 16

# Restraining Order

**ZION HAS A FOURTEEN-DAY BOOK TOUR.** Lord knows I was going to miss him. But I needed this time to complete the manuscript for my book. I am planning to meet him when he gets to Miami though, which is about day seven or eight. I don't know if he can be alone in that city. He told me how women throw themselves at him and are willing to do whatever, whenever, and wherever. I would like to think that he can handle himself accordingly but I don't know. I'm sure he is tempted at times.

After working on my book for two days straight, I needed a break. I called Natasha and Dianne to see if they were in the mood to go out for a drink. So much has been going on in all of our lives that we haven't been hanging out much lately. They both agreed that a girl's night out would be good for all of us. It was a Friday night so we arranged to meet at Jaspers. Normally we would go to Jaspers for brunch on Sundays, but occasionally we would go there on Fridays. It was like being at a club for happy hour on Fridays. This way we could get the club feel without actually being at a club.

As soon as we were seated at our table, I noticed Taye at the bar. My initial instinct was to leave and go to another spot, but I was determined not to let him ruin my evening out with the girls. I was hoping that he wouldn't notice me.

We ordered appetizers and drinks. Natasha was almost six months pregnant so she ordered a virgin strawberry daiquiri. While we were waiting, Dianne told us that Nihya's mother passed away and she was being sexually abused.

"Nelson is not taking this well at all. He got so upset that he cursed me out and started breaking stuff in our family room," Dianne said, with a sad look on her face. "I never thought that my husband would ever hit me, but at that moment I wasn't so sure anymore. I was actually afraid of him. I didn't like it at all."

"Well it's a good thing he didn't. I'm sure his emotions got the best of him, but unfortunately, that's how people end up hurt or dead. But thank goodness he snapped out of it," I said to Dianne, not really knowing what else to say.

"How is Nihya doing?" Natasha asked.

"She is such a strong little girl, but of course she is having a hard time. She pretty much cries herself to sleep every night. Normally I go in the room with her until she falls asleep. "

"Unfortunately, I can relate," Natasha said, as her eyes began to water.

I was glad that our appetizers came because I really wanted to change the subject. I was starting to feel bad because I don't really speak to my mother and both Natasha and Dianne had lost their mother at an early age. I was closer to my father but he died a few years ago from colon cancer. Although I was grown at the time, it was still very painful. I was always daddy's girl. I never understood why my mother treated me so mean. It was as if she was jealous of her own daughter. She would do things for my brother that she would never do for me. So when our parents divorced, I went to live with our father and my brother stayed with our mother.

"What's wrong Lynda?" Dianne asked obviously noticing that my mind was somewhere else.

"Nothing, I was thinking about my father and how much I miss him." I never mention my mother around Dianne because she would try to convince me to make amends with her. She doesn't seem to understand that I don't have a problem with my mother. My mother never seemed to love me and that really hurts.

At that moment, Natasha raised her glass and said, "Well ladies, let's toast to our friendship. Without my girls, I don't know where I would be."

"I'll drink to that," Dianne and I both said, as we tapped our glasses together, making that clinking noise.

"Lynda, how is that manuscript coming along?" Dianne asked.

"It's coming along okay. I am not making the progress I would like to make, but it's coming along nicely. Sometimes I can't concentrate because I'm thinking about Zion."

"Girl, I haven't seen you this much into one guy in I don't know when," Natasha added.

"I know, and believe me it's tripping me out too."

"Isn't that Taye coming this way?" Dianne asked seemingly unsure if that was actually Taye.

"Lord, say it isn't so," I said out loud hoping he was not coming over to our table. But sure enough, he was.

"Ladies, do you mind if I join you?"

"Well, actually this is supposed to be ladies night out so I kind of do mind," I said, with an attitude.

"What about you two ladies, do you mind?" Taye said, looking at Natasha and Dianne. The way he was slurring with his words, he obviously had too much to drink.

"Taye, please. We are in the middle of an important conversation. Could you leave us alone so we can continue?" This time I asked nicely thinking maybe he would leave without a hassle.

"Lynda, this muthafucking restaurant doesn't belong to you so I can sit where I please. If you don't like it maybe you should leave so I can talk to your friends."

Taye always seemed like a gentleman so his behavior was startling to me. I couldn't understand why he was being so mean. We agreed to go our separate ways. The manager must have noticed Taye's aggression so he came over to ask us if we were okay.

"Actually, this gentleman is bothering us and I would like it if he left our table."

"Oh it's like that? Okay. I got you. I will leave these ladies alone. Sorry if I caused a disturbance," Taye said, as he left our table and went back over to the bar.

I was so embarrassed and ready to leave. "I'm sorry, I didn't mean for this girl's night out to turn out like this," I said, with my eyes beginning to water.

"Don't worry about it girl. I need to go home and check on Nelson anyway. Nihya is with her grandmother for the night," Dianne said, as she left money for the entire bill. "It's my treat tonight. Come on, let's go."

"Thanks Di," Natasha responded. "I'm so tired. I can't wait to lay this big belly down."

As we left Jaspers, I could feel eyes looking at me. I'm sure a pair of those eyes belonged to Taye. The tears began to fall from my eyes as we walked to our cars.

"Lynda, are you going to be okay?" Natasha asked with genuine concern.

"Yeah, I can't believe Taye is acting like this. I wish Zion was here because I really don't want to be alone."

"Do you want me to come over after I check on Nelson?"

"No, but thank you. You already have enough on your plate. I do appreciate it though," I said, trying to control my tears.

"Well call me if you need me. "

"I'll call you when I get home," I told Dianne.

"Me too," Natasha added.

Calling Dianne was a routine for us after a girl's night out. It was a security measure to make sure we all made it home safely. On my way home, I called Zion from my cell phone, but he did not answer. I began to cry harder. I don't know why but I was beginning to feel insecure about my relationship with Zion. I didn't like him being on the road with access to all those women. Maybe I was in over my head with this relationship. He told me that I could travel with him, but I have to learn to trust him. I wonder if he even trusts me.

Before I pulled into my neighborhood, my cell phone rang. The incoming call said Heaven, so I knew it was Zion. I tried to get myself together before I answered the phone, so he wouldn't know I had been crying.

"Hey, Zion, how are you?"

"What's the matter baby?" I guess he could hear in my voice that I was crying.

"I'm okay. "

"You sure, you sound upset."

"No, I'm tired."

"I'm tired myself. But things are going very well. The books are selling like hotcakes."

"That's great, Zion, I'm so proud of you. I know you are probably tired of me saying that. But, I am so happy for you."

"No, I'm not tired of you saying that. It's actually nice to hear those words," Zion said, with a smile in his voice. "I miss you."

"I miss you, too."

"I love you and I'll call you tomorrow."

"I love you, too, Zion. Goodnight."

Before I get out of my car, I always make sure I have my keys in my hand. As I approach my door, I heard a car door slam. When I turned around, I couldn't believe my eyes. It was Taye.

"So is that how it's going to be when I see you in public? You act like I'm bothering you."

"Taye, listen. Let's not do this tonight. I don't like to talk to you when you are like this."

"Like what?"

"Obviously you are drunk."

"Well how about you sober me up?" he said, trying to kiss me.

*When I'm Loving You*

"Come on Taye, please stop it."

"You want me to stop? Not long ago you were begging for me to put it in."

"I'm seeing someone else now." After the words came out of my mouth, I instantly regret saying them.

"Oh, okay. I get it. You needed space from me to start seeing someone else."

"No, that's not it. I left you both alone back then." Once again, I regretted letting those words come out.

"What the fuck do you mean, left us *both* alone?"

"Taye, please, I can't do this out here."

"Well let's talk inside then." I opened my door and let him in. I would soon regret that too. I see this night was going to be full of regrets.

Once inside, Taye grabbed me by my arms. He had such a tight grip on them.

"Taye, you are hurting me, let me go. We can talk if you let me go."

"Oh I don't want to talk now," he said, as he grabbed my pants, trying to unbutton them. I tried fighting him off, but it was no use. Taye was out of control. When he succeeded at getting my pants down, he pulled his pants down and pulled out his penis, which was already hard. He began stroking it before he put it inside of me. As he penetrated me, he whispered in my ear, "You are my girl and you are going to have my baby."

At that moment, I realized that Taye was inside of me with no condom. All I could do was cry and beg for him to stop before he did something that he would regret. But then I could feel him throbbing so I knew he was about to ejaculate. I could not believe this was happening to me. All I could think of was my relationship with Zion, how much I loved him and how I did not want to lose him.

Taye pulled out of me and let his cum squirt out in his hand. I guess he must have realized what he was doing and the evidence he would leave behind inside of me. When he was done, he got up and pulled his pants up with one hand still holding his cum in the other.

"No need to go crying rape because everyone knows that we were once a couple. And tell your little boyfriend thanks for keeping *my* pussy loose for me but his time is up," he said, as he went into the bathroom and washed his hands. "We're getting back together."

This ordeal with Taye lasted about fifteen minutes so I checked my cell phone to see if Dianne called. If I don't call her within a certain timeframe, she will call me. I had one missed call from her so I called her back.

"Girl I was beginning to worry about you," Dianne said, as she answered the phone.

I couldn't say anything. I cried.

"Lynda, what's wrong? Never mind, I'm on my way," Dianne hung up before I could get the words out.

Taye left when I told him that Dianne was on her way over. I made him believe that we already had plans and that she went home to change her clothes.

"Taye, if I cancel now she will suspect something is wrong and come over anyway. That's how Dianne is," I said, hoping that he would believe my story and leave without hurting me physically. The emotional scars were already there.

He was so angry that I thought he was going to hit me. But, he stormed out of the door. Before he left he said, "I am trying to love you and I don't know why you won't let me. We had a good thing so I don't understand what the problem is now. It must be that dude you're seeing, but I see that's going to have to end one way or another."

When Dianne arrived, she used the emergency key I had given her. I was still sitting in the same place. She sat down next me to and asked what happened. I relived what seemed like the longest fifteen minutes of my life. She cried with me. I could tell that she was tired of everything that was going on around her. I wasn't sure if I was going to press charges but I felt that I should get a restraining order against him. He was becoming more and more violent which I didn't see coming until now. I don't think he is used to being rejected by women so he is not handling our breakup very well.

I didn't know how I was going to break this to Zion. I thought about not telling him but this wasn't something you kept a secret from someone you are trying to build a future with. I really don't want to put him in the middle of my madness. Would he even believe my story? Maybe if I agreed not to press charges, Taye would leave me alone and all this could go away. Now I am going to have to make sure I keep up with my HIV tests every six months. I'm glad the hospitals now give the Plan B, which is the morning after birth control pill. I decided to go there in the morning in case some of Taye's semen was released inside of me before he pulled out. I definitely could not go through with another abortion.

## Chapter 17

# Close Call

**ZION AND I ARE BECOMING REALLY SERIOUS.** We spend so much time over each other's place that it would make since for us to move in together, but we agreed that we would keep our separate places until we were ready to take our relationship a step further, which is marriage. Dianne teases us and calls us Martin and Gina. I love Zion so much that I hate when we don't spend the night together. Normally the only time we don't spend the night together is when he has a book tour. Sometimes I go with him, but I don't want to smother him so I make sure I give him enough space.

One day, Zion and I returned from a weekend trip to New York and someone had slashed the tires on my car and broke out the back window. I was so upset that I dropped down to the ground.

"Baby, do you know who would do this to you?" Zion asked as he helped me up.

"I don't know offhand. I haven't done anything to anyone that I know of Zion," I lied, as I immediately thought about Taye's threats.

I couldn't think of anyone who would have wanted to hurt me other than Taye. I really didn't think it would have been Maurice because he is the one who didn't want to be in a relationship with me. Marlon was now married so I couldn't imagine him doing this. Then I thought maybe it had to be Taye but there was no proof. Could Zion have a jealous ex-girlfriend who may have done this? But I didn't share that thought.

"Zion, I think maybe Taye did this to my car but I don't know why he would do that. We haven't been together in a while. He should have moved on by now."

"Maybe he realized that he wasn't over you. When was the last time you talked to him?"

I wasn't sure how to answer Zion's question because I never told him what Taye did to me that time while he was on his book tour. He would be so angry with me if I told him now because I kept this from him. I'm sure this will come out sooner or later but right now I thought later would be better.

"We should call the police to report the vandalism to your car."

After I filed the police report, I started thinking about some strange calls that I had been getting off and on for the past few months. I really didn't think it was Taye harassing me because he seemed to have too much to lose. Maybe I was wrong. I couldn't prove it was Taye though. Now that Zion had a book on the shelf, maybe he has a jealous stalker that wants me out of the way. Unsure of who it was, I was beginning to get scared.

"Zion, maybe we should stay at your house tonight. I don't feel safe here."

"Sure baby, get some clothes and we can go."

"Okay."

As soon as we pulled off and headed up Southern Avenue, a car sped up behind us. I was so scared. If Taye or someone was going to hurt me, I didn't want Zion to be hurt because of me.

"Zion, what are we going to do? I think that car is following us." I couldn't tell what kind of car it was because it was dark outside.

"Lynda, calm down. I'm going to go towards the police station on Alabama Avenue and maybe we would lose whoever is following us."

That's when I heard gunshots. This was getting serious and I had never been so terrified in all of my life. Getting closer to the police station, the car sped by us. Zion put on his high beams and managed to get the tag number of the car.

"Zion, did a bullet hit your car?" I asked, relieved that the car passed us.

"I don't know, but let's go and report this right now to the police. I have the tag number of the car."

I began to feel tingling in my feet. "Zion, something is not right. My feet are tingling."

Zion looked at the back seat of his car and noticed a small hole on the side behind the passenger seat. He looked as if he had seen a ghost. "Lynda, baby, lean forward."

"Why Zion?" I started crying.

Apparently, I had been hit by one of the bullets. It traveled through the trunk of his car and hit me in the back. Zion turned back around and went back on Southern Avenue towards Greater Southeast Hospital. He was trying to drive and calm me down at the same time. I was hysterical. Although I didn't feel any pain, my feet were still tingling so I was scared. I heard that sometimes numbness start with your feet and move up your legs, and I didn't want either, and possibly becoming paralyzed. When we arrived to the emergency room, I tried to get out of the car and walk.

"Lynda, please don't get out. Let me go and get help."

A few doctors came out of the emergency room doors. One of them had a wheelchair. *Damn, is it that serious* I thought to myself. It must have been because when they realized it was an injury to my back, they went back and returned with a stretcher to lay me on. *Lord, please help me.* I said a silent prayer for strength. The crazy thing about the whole incident is that I didn't even know I was shot. Not only did it not hurt, I didn't bleed. I found out later from the police that the bullet traveled through the trunk of the car and because Zion had so much stuff in there, the bullet slowed down so I caught the tail end of the blow. So in a way, Zion saved my life.

In the emergency room, I couldn't help but think of my family and friends. I wondered how people would have reacted if I would have died. I thought about what Zion must be going through right about now. I ended up having to be sent by helicopter to Washington Hospital Center. Apparently, the better doctors, for gun shot wounds to the back, were at that hospital. I was hit less than an inch from my spine so not only was I lucky to be walking around, I was blessed to be still alive.

*When I'm Loving You*

After a series of test to make sure there wasn't any internal damage, I was exhausted. Zion was at the hospital the entire time. I didn't know that he had called Natasha and Dianne. They were also there with Tyrone and Nelson, respectively. I managed to finally get some rest. At first, I was so scared to fall asleep because I didn't want to lose any feeling in my legs while I was sleep. When I woke up, the whole crew was in the hospital room with me. There was so much love in the room. Zion also called my brother who was traveling making a documentary. He said that she would notify the rest of the family to let them know that I had a close call but I was okay. Although my mother and I weren't really speaking, she called me to make sure I didn't want her to come. I didn't think it was necessary; no need being phony.

While we were joking around, a police officer walked into the room. "Ms. Lynda Davis?"

"Yes officer?"

"I'm Officer Murphy. Which one of you is Zion Jones?"

"I am officer," Zion said, nervously.

I would like to speak with the two of you. Could the rest of you wait in the hall, please?"

"Sure officer," my friends said, almost in unison.

"I was able to trace the tag number of the car that you reported was following you," the officer said to Zion. "Do either of you know a Taylor Dixon?"

"Taye?" I began to cry. "I don't understand. Why would he want to hurt me? We agreed not to see each other anymore. I thought he moved on."

"Is he in custody officer?" Zion asked obviously concerned about my safety.

"Actually, he's dead."

"Dead?" I asked in total amazement.

"Yes ma'am. When officers went to question him, he tried to elude the police. He was speeding, lost control of his car, and hit a utility pole. He wasn't wearing his seatbelt so he was thrown from the car and pronounced dead at the scene."

"This is too much for me right now," I said, pulling the covers up to my shoulders. "I guess he can't hurt me now."

"No ma'am, he cannot."

That goes to show that although some people seem like their lives are together, you never know what a person is going through. Of course, I was glad that Taye couldn't hurt me anymore, but I was also sad because I cared about him. Even though, we were going in different directions with our lives. We didn't really argue or anything. I guess Taye wasn't honest about how he felt about us going our separate ways. He told me that he was fine with the situation. I never told Zion about the threatening phone calls because I couldn't prove it was Taye.

The first night was terrible in the hospital. I couldn't get comfortable. I couldn't lie on my back, side or stomach without being in pain. Not to mention I was already scared to go to sleep because I was afraid of waking up without feeling in my legs. When I did manage to fall asleep, I kept having nightmares and would wake up screaming. I called Zion. He didn't want to leave me anyway but I thought I would be okay. He talked to me until my eyes were heavy and I fell asleep on the phone. When I woke up, Zion was still holding the other end of the phone. He was snoring in the phone.

"Zion, baby, wake up. It's morning."

"Good morning, sweetheart. Did you get some rest?"

"Yes, baby. Thank you for staying on the phone with me last night."

"No problem, Lynda, you're my baby, anything I can do to help you through this I will. I wish you didn't have to go through this. I wish I could have protected you."

"It's okay, Zion, I'm glad that you didn't get hurt in the process. I wouldn't have been able to live with myself if you got hurt because of me. I love you. See you in a few hours."

The following night, the hospital staff allowed Zion to stay in my room. I was going home the next day anyway but I had to make it through another night. They were going to keep me for one more night for observation. Zion slept in the chair next to my bed. He looked so uncomfortable but I didn't want him to leave me. I had been through some serious trauma and I didn't want to be alone. I needed him, he was willing to be there for me, and I loved him even more. In the middle of the night, I was having severe back pains. Zion heard me crying so he sat on the edge of the hospital bed.

"Lynda, what's wrong? Are you in pain?" he asked gently rubbing my back

"Yes, I'm in so much pain, but I took a couple of pain pills. I have to wait for it to kick in though," I said, with tears in my eyes. *I hope this isn't an indication of what I have to look forward to for the rest of my life,* I thought to myself as Zion continued massaging my back. I thought this because the doctor said that they were not going to remove the bullet. It was lodged too close to my spine and it would probably cause me more harm than good to remove it.

Once the Tylenol with codeine kicked in, Zion asked if there was anything else he could do for me.

"Could you massage my feet and legs for me?"

"Are you feeling numbness again, if so I can get the nurse?"

"No, I think a massage would help make me feel better."

"Okay, sure no problem, baby."

Zion began to massage my feet. He loved my feet so he spent extra time massaging and caressing them. Occasionally he would kiss my toes. He massaged my feet like the Chinese woman when she does my pedicure, but then, he sucked my big toe. He sucked the left big toe and then he did the same thing to the right. *Lord, don't let that nurse walk in here right now.* I thought to myself as I started getting moist. Zion continued massaging my feet and then moved to my legs. He didn't spend much time on my legs as it seems he was anxious to move up to my thighs.

Zion sat on the left side of the hospital bed while still caressing my thigh. I received a famous wet but not too sloppy Zion kiss. I love those kisses from him. It does something to me! I didn't have on any panties so he had easy access to my pussy. Still sitting on my left, Zion took his left hand and reached between my legs until he felt my moisture.

He moaned deeply, "Ummm."

I moaned softly, "oooohh Zion."

*Lord, don't let that nurse walk in here right now.* I thought to myself again but this time on the verge of an orgasm. I loved the way Zion finger fucked me. He would use his middle finger and the pointer to insert inside of me while his thumb would gently massage my clit. That was some serious finger control. I loved it!

Being fingered so nicely in addition to that wet kiss from

Zion, my juices flowed all over his hand. *How are we going to explain this wet spot to the nurse?* After Zion ensured I was finished cumming, he retrieved a towel from the bathroom to put under me, as well as a soapy washcloth in order to clean me up. I love him! Zion's erection suggested that he had some semen that he wanted to release.

"Zion do you want me to jerk you off?"

"Naw, baby, I'll be alright. I don't know if I want the nurse or doctor to come in here and my dick be in your hand," he said, laughing.

"Okay, but let me know if you change your mind," I responded laughing with him.

Zion kissed me gently on my lips and then sat back in the chair. I knew he was still horny because his erection had not subsided. I would definitely have to make it up to him later. I hope this bullet in my back doesn't affect my sexual performance. I want to be able to keep riding all of Zion's nine inches and without holding on.

When I was released from the hospital the next morning, Zion took me to his place to relax. He knew that if I was at my place then I would feel compelled to clean up or lift something that I am not supposed to. At his house, I could get the rest that I really needed. I knew I would be in great hands.

CHAPTER 18

# Justice of the Peace

**AFTER TYRONE PROPOSED TO ME,** I suggested we attend marriage counseling before we jumped the broom. Yes, I love him, but I don't think anyone should get married without seeking professional advice. He told me that he didn't go to counseling before he married Annie, so he agreed to my suggestion.

The counseling sessions were not only about us getting married, it was also about dealing with Aisha's death. I wanted to make sure I was marrying Tyrone for the right reasons and not because I was grieving the loss of our daughter. The counselor I chose knew about the tragedy we suffered so she thought it would be good for Tyrone and me to join a support group of other parents who also lost their children. The first day of the support group was very hard. Listening to stories of how some children were missing and found dead, and some died of childhood diseases, pierced my heart. There were also a few single parents there who had lost their children at the hands of the other parent. I really can't imagine someone killing their own child, but anyone who watches the news knows this sort of thing is not unusual.

After the third support group session, I began to discuss, openly, the loss of Aisha. Tyrone still wasn't quite comfortable sharing his personal feelings with people he didn't know. Since I was able to talk about Aisha's death with other people that could honestly relate to losing a child, I felt a lot better. Sometimes it's easy to feel that we are alone in what we are going through. But no parent should ever have to bury his or her child.

One of the most important questions our marriage counselor asked us is if there was anything that we haven't told the other because we shouldn't begin our marriage with any secrets. I immediately thought about what I read in Aisha's diary. I needed to share what I read with Tyrone.

∾ ∾ ∾ ∾ ∾

Tyrone and I decided to get married at the Justice of the Peace. I really wasn't in the mood to plan the lavish wedding I always dreamed of since I was a little girl. At first, it bothered me that I wasn't having the "wedding of the year," but then I realized that what was most important was to become Tyrone's wife. Not to mention I was about seven months pregnant and waddling down the aisle wasn't my idea of a lavish wedding.

After reading the letters that Tyrone wrote over ten years ago, but never sent to me, there was no doubt in my mind that I wanted to marry him. I love him so much that I can't imagine my world without him now that we are reunited. I'm glad God has given us a second chance at love.

We decided to get married on the day that it was confirmed I was pregnant wish Aisha. I knew the exact date because I still had the sonogram picture from my first doctor's visit. That day was very special for me because that was the day that Tyrone said someday I would be his wife. I guess someday is finally here. I know Tyrone and I were only kids when I had gotten pregnant but he was so ecstatic when I showed him the sonogram picture of our baby growing inside of me. I thought his mother would be upset because after all, we were having sex in her house. But she wasn't upset. Although she allowed me to live with them, she made sure we learned to be responsible for our baby. I wish Tyrone's mother could be here for our marriage. She always wanted us to get back together like Aisha did.

The day that I was to marry Tyrone was so beautiful outside. The sun was shining and it was low humidity. I was glad because the extra weight I was carrying made it feel hotter outside than it actually was. I decided to wear a cream-colored maternity sundress because I dare not wear white. Dianne was my matron of honor, although I wasn't having a traditional wedding, and Lynda was my maid of honor. I'm so glad that Lynda had a smooth recovery after being shot. She is definitely a walking angel. To look at her, you wouldn't know that anything had happened to her.

Dianne and Lynda decided to wear matching cream sundresses with peach flowers on them. So I guess my wedding colors were peaches and cream. Dianne and Lynda were escorted by Nelson and Zion, respectively. The plan was for me to meet Tyrone at the court building so we could exchange our marriage vows. Although our wedding was not a traditional ceremony, I wanted it be special.

When I arrived at the justice of the peace, Tyrone was standing there waiting for me. It was really like a scene from an urban fairytale. He was wearing a nice black suit and he was looking very handsome and extremely sexy. I couldn't wait for the honeymoon to begin, seven months pregnant and all.

Tyrone and I wrote our own vows. When Tyrone grabbed my hand and looked me in the eyes, I instantly began to cry. Tyrone wasn't a man of many words so whatever words he spoke really meant something.

"Natasha, I don't know where to begin. I have loved you since we were sixteen years old. God is giving me a second chance at love with you and I promise I'll always be there for you. You know I am not a man of many words, but words could never express what I feel in my heart anyway. God made you for me, as he made Eve for Adam, from my rib. I always want you beside me, for better or for worse. As your husband, I will love and cherish you until I take my last breath."

When it was my turn to take my vow, I could barely speak. "Tyrone, you told me a very long time ago that someday I would be your wife. Today is that day and I am so happy that we have been given this second chance at true unconditional love. I know everything happens for a reason. I trust in the Lord, with all my heart, so I know this is the path that I am supposed to take. On this day, seventeen years ago, I found out that I was going to be the mother of your child and I was so very happy. Although our daughter Aisha has gone to be with the Lord, she will live forever in our hearts. As your wife, I will love and cherish you until I take my last breath." By this time, everyone, including the men, was crying.

Tyrone and I had already agreed that no matter what we said in our vows, that we would end it with the same line. When we were pronounced man and wife, Tyrone kissed me and rubbed my stomach. The baby kicked, responding to his touch. It's really amazing how a bond can be created with a baby in the womb.

We all left the court building holding on to our significant others. The weather was still beautiful. Before I could get completely out of the door, I felt a hard blow to my stomach and I fell to the ground. Tyrone grabbed me, Zion grabbed Lynda and before anyone could stop her, Dianne grabbed Annie. Where did Annie come from? How did she know we would be here today?

As I laid on the ground in disbelief, I realized that Annie had kicked me in my stomach. I'm assuming in attempts to ruin my pregnancy and my wedding day. Tyrone, fearing that the baby could be in danger, called 911 from his cell phone. He was so concerned about the baby that he never even acknowledged Annie. He didn't have to because Dianne had pushed Annie to the ground and was punching her in the face and banging her head on the ground. I had never seen anyone beat someone's ass while wearing three and a half-inch heel shoes. Normally, it would have been Lynda who would have gone after her, but Zion refused to let her go since she was still recovering from the gunshot wound. But, trust me; she was trying to get away from Zion's grip.

When the ambulance arrived, the paramedics put me on the stretcher. Tyrone was crying and cursing. He swore that he would go after Annie if something happens to his child. Tyrone and I had already lost one child. I don't think neither one of us could handle losing another one.

On the way to the hospital, I started having contractions. I couldn't believe it; I was going into premature labor. This was supposed to be one of the happiest days of my life, the day I was marrying my soul mate. Was God trying to tell me something? If my baby dies, Annie won't have to worry about Tyrone or going to jail, for involuntary manslaughter, or whatever her charge would be. However, she would most certainly die in any manner that I chose.

Fortunately, at the hospital, the doctors were able to stop my contractions. They told me that they were going to keep me in the hospital overnight for observations. They also mentioned that I would probably have to be on bed rest for the rest of my pregnancy. Tyrone and I were relieved that our baby wasn't going to be born premature and we prayed that the blow to my stomach wouldn't cause any long-term affect for my baby or me.

Nelson, Lynda and Zion came by the hospital to see me later on that night, before visiting hours were over.

"Where is Dianne?" I asked looking at Nelson who I could tell had been crying.

"In Jail." Nelson looked at the floor with his hand in his pocket.

"Jail?" I screamed.

"Yeah when the police got there, Dianne would not let Annie go at all. I think she would have beaten her to death if the police hadn't shown up. Did you all know that Dianne was so strong? I couldn't even get her off that girl."

"Yeah Dianne and I took a few self defense classes," Lynda

responded. "When I dropped out of the class, Dianne kept going so who knows what type of techniques she had learned."

"I called my lawyer and he suggested that we try to get Annie to drop the charges against Dianne. But that would mean that you would probably have to not press charges against Annie," Nelson said, almost pleading to me. "But my lawyer also said that since Dianne doesn't have any priors she would do community service at most or serve a few months probation for her assault charge."

"Nelson, don't worry. Anything for Dianne. After all, she was defending me," I said, with a partial smile. *Dianne did promise to always have my back*, I thought to myself as I drifted of to sleep.

## Chapter 19

# A Fresh Start

**SOON AFTER NIHYA'S MOTHER WAS BURIED,** the man that she believed to be her father all these years, committed suicide. I'm sure Walter committed suicide because he knew that sooner or later the truth about what he did to Nihya would come out. I'm sure he was also having a hard time with losing Marie. Life can be full of pain sometimes, but we can't allow these struggles to take over and defeat us. We need to start making wiser choices and consider the consequences up front.

Nihya's grandmother didn't feel we should tell her the truth about the suicide but that Walter died from a heart attack. She felt that maybe Nihya would feel guilty that he killed himself because she told what he did to her. I didn't like lying to Nihya but I agreed with her grandmother that she didn't need to carry that kind of guilt with her. She was already carrying around too much as it is for someone her age.

I can't believe that I've been to a funeral, a wedding, and to jail all in one month. This is too much for me. Annie didn't press charges against me because she didn't want Natasha to press charges against her. Nelson was so disappointed in me, but I was more disappointed in myself. I don't know what came over me. It was almost as if I was having an out-of-body experience, but I'm ashamed to say it felt good. I hadn't been in a fistfight since my sister and I fought over ten years ago. On that day, I promised that I wouldn't allow anyone to get me so upset to the point where I had to resort to a physical altercation. And here I was fighting outside of a court building.

I know Nelson left me in jail longer than I had to stay on purpose. He could have gotten me out immediately but he waited for several hours. He often told me that holding things inside and acting as if I had things under control would, at some point, lead to violent behaviors. Everyone always seems to need me so I often don't have an outlet for myself, except for Nelson. I don't open up to him much for fear of possibly pushing him away with my problems. But if I don't get a handle on some of my own deep-rooted issues, I may eventually push him away.

Realizing I can't be my own therapist, I am now seeing someone else that I can talk to regarding how I feel about my mother's death. I have grown up with abandonment issues; a fear that people would leave me like she did so I've been scared to get close to other people. Getting married was a huge step for me and I don't even think my friends realize how afraid I was to get close to them as well. Then the miscarriage I had in my early twenties doesn't help my issues either.

People frown upon therapy, but I don't know why. It's really helpful to have someone outside of your situation to talk to;

someone who has an unbiased opinion on what's going on in your life. Nelson is also seeing a therapist to help him with not only his new role as a father, but a father of an abused daughter. Sometimes he is scared to let her out of his sight if there are other men around.

Nihya is seeing her own child psychologist. Although that is my field of expertise, there are things that she may not want to share with me since I am her stepmother. It's a conflict of interest for clients to be friends or family. I am really amazed as to how well Nihya has adjusted to living with Nelson and me. She is a joy to have around. She visits her grandmother, Marie's mother, every other weekend so they can continue the close bond that they have. No one in Walter's family wants anything to do with her now that they know she is not a blood relative. Plus I think some of them suspected Walter was abusing her and they probably don't want to deal with that guilt. Of course, this is all my speculation.

As for me having a baby, I didn't think it was a good time for us to add a new addition to our family. Nelson disagrees so we are seeing a marriage counselor about that situation. In the meantime, I've agreed not to resume wearing the birth control patch. If it's God's plan for me to become pregnant then so be it. I've trusted God this far so why stop now.

For our fifth wedding anniversary, Nelson asked me to marry him again. He said that he wanted us to renew our vows since Nihya is a part of our family. He knows that one of the main reasons I found him to be a good catch is because he didn't have any kids. I guess he wanted to make sure I'm still willing to be there for better or worse. I love Nihya but I don't need anymore surprise children showing up at our door.

## Chapter 20

# The Beginning of an End

**THIS HAS BEEN TRULY AN EMOTIONAL YEAR.** Not a day goes by that I don't think about Taye and the fact that he tried to kill me. He seemed to have so much to live for, so I don't understand why he would jeopardize all that to kill me. On top of that, I'm not sure where Zion and I are going with our relationship. At times, it seems as if we are progressing and then other times, it feels like we are stagnant. Love is confusing.

One day, while I was praying, I asked God to give me a sign that Zion and I were meant to be together. The very next day, I ran into Justin; the one I let get away. I knew seeing him was a test, but I failed the moment I looked into Justin's eyes and they told me he was not happy in his marriage. As any friend would, I was going to be there for him anyway he needed me to be. It was evident that Justin and I still had feelings for each other because when we embraced, we didn't let go right away. It felt damn good being in his arms again.

"Well if it isn't Ms. Lynda Davis. Or should I ask if it's still *Ms. Davis*?"

"Hey Justin, it's good to see you. And yes, it's still *Ms. Davis,*" I answered still in his embrace.

"It could have been Mrs. Palmer."

"Davis-Palmer maybe," was the only response I could come up with as I eased out of his arms.

"How are things with you?"

"Life is good, no complaints really." I didn't feel like going into details at that moment. "How have things been with you and yours?"

Justin hesitated before responding. "Okay, I guess."

We stared into each other's eyes for a few moments, not sure what to say next. I could sense that something was bothering Justin, but I wasn't going to press the issue. The moment became awkward. Then Justin broke the silence.

"How is your book coming along?"

"Actually it's coming along nicely. I'm just adding a few final changes. I had a few setbacks in my schedule, but everything is working out fine now."

"That's good. I'm happy things are coming together for you. I know you've wanted this for so long."

"Yeah, it's a dream that's finally coming true. It's nothing like doing something that you are passionate about. Sometimes I wish you were patient enough to be there for me."

"I know and I'm sorry, Lynda."

"Don't be. I know you wanted a family and I didn't expect you to wait for me, although I wanted you to. I loved you."

"I know you did. Believe me, I somewhat regret the choice I made. I mean I love my kids, but their mother and I don't really get along. We just coexist for the kids."

"Justin, that's not a healthy relationship."

"I know but I'm not going to walk out on my girls."

"I can respect that, but what about you and your happiness?"

"I guess that doesn't matter as long as my daughters are happy."

Justin stood there with his hands in his pockets and looking at the ground. Standing before me was a broken man committed to his family. There are so many people in this same situation and I don't understand how people can function in such dysfunction.

"Justin, I'm sorry about your situation. You are a good man and you deserve to be happy; however, only you can control that. My cell phone number is still the same if you ever want to talk." I handed him my card in case he doesn't have my number anymore.

"Thanks Lynda. Don't be surprised if you hear from me very soon."

"I won't be." I kissed Justin on his cheek and then walked away. I couldn't stand there another second seeing him like that. Although I still love Justin, I have moved on. I'm in love with Zion and I want him to be my future.

Over the next few days, I avoided Justin's calls. I was afraid that I was going to start falling for him again and I don't need the distraction. Men have always been a damn distraction in my life. Zion is starting to notice my distance from him so I think it is best that I let Justin know I'm in a relationship. I don't want to mess things up with Zion, again.

I agreed to meet Justin one weekend when I knew Zion would be out of town. Justin gave me an address where to meet him. I assumed it was an apartment of one of his friends or a family member until I got inside. The items inside and the way it was decorated suggested that Justin lived in the apartment.

"Justin, you live here?"

"It's a long story."

"Well, looks like I have time if you do."

He let out a deep sigh and explained how his wife filed for a divorce but they had to be legally separated for six months first. He is renting an apartment to show the courts that they are separated on paper; however, he would still spend most of the time at their home so the girls wouldn't know what was going on. He would leave at night after the girls go to sleep and go back to the house in the morning when it was time to get them ready for school. Now how is that for dysfunction?

"Justin, how long do you think you will be able to keep this from your daughters?"

"I don't know but I figured it was worth a try for their sake."

"Sounds crazy to me, but what I think doesn't matter."

"It does matter."

"Why does it matter?"

"Because I want to be with you."

"Justin, we can't be together. I am in a relationship and you are still married."

"I didn't know you were in a relationship."

"Well I am. Besides, your situation is too much drama for me. I got enough going on already."

I explained to Justin all that has happened in my life for the past year including the drama with Natasha and Dianne. I emphasized that I was still trying to deal with the emotional trauma of Taye trying to kill me, and the fact that Taye forced himself on me while he was in a drunken rage.

"That is a lot to deal with. Lynda, I'm sorry. I didn't know."

"Of course you didn't know so there isn't a need to be sorry."

"I really miss you. I miss us."

"Well Justin, you made your choice. You can't expect me to run back to you after all this time as if I haven't found someone and moved on with my life."

"I know. You're right. Do you miss me at all?"

"Of course I miss you or I wouldn't be here right now. I miss you but I love Zion."

"The author, Zion?"

"Yeah, how did you know?"

"I didn't. I just figured you would end up with someone in your field; someone who understands and supports your dreams."

"Come on Justin, don't do this. Don't make it seem like I am the one who left you."

"No, you didn't leave me, but you wouldn't tell me how you felt."

"It was too complicated at the time, but you knew I loved you."

"I loved you too. I actually still do," Justin said as he pulled me onto his lap.

"Justin, don't."

"Don't what?"

He kissed me on my neck as he massaged my breast. My pussy pulsated as I became moist. I could feel Justin becoming hard. I wanted him so badly, but I knew it wouldn't be a good idea to have sex with him. However, my thoughts couldn't keep up with my actions. Before I knew it, he was finger fucking me so good that stopping him was not an option. It's a shame I don't remember how my clothes came off, but I do remember cumming all over his hand.

"Justin, I don't think we should go any further."

"I had a feeling you were going to say that."

"This ain't right. I hope you are not disappointed."
"She says, after cumming all over my hand."
"Stop being sarcastic."
"Come on let me make love to you tonight."
"No, it will only complicate things."
"I think it's too late for that."
"Why you say that?'
"Because you still on top of me."

I eased off Justin's lap and gathered my clothes. Guilt filled my being and my eyes began to water. I deliberately avoided Justin's eyes as I dressed. As tears fell from my eyes, I could feel Justin looking at me. I was still afraid to see the expression on his face, so I continued to avoid eye contact.

"Lynda, before you go, I want to say I'm sorry for putting you in this situation."

"I can't blame you. I should have known better." My tears were uncontrollable at this point. I didn't know whether I was crying because I love Zion, and I pretty much cheated on him, or because I was losing Justin, once again.

ᴦ ᴦ ᴦ ᴦ ᴦ

Over the next several weeks, Justin called almost everyday. I let all of his calls go to voicemail. I continued to stay with Zion, partially because I didn't want to be home in case Justin decided to show up at my house. Zion was back in town, but I was glad he had a busy schedule. It gave me time to clear my thoughts of Justin. After checking the message Justin left, I decided that it was time to let Justin go completely. I considered changing my phone number, if it became necessary. The bottom line is, Justin made his choice and it wasn't me. No matter what, he is forever connected to his wife because of his daughters. I simply couldn't be a part of his life.

I decided to write Justin a good-bye letter and mail it to his apartment. The letter I wrote was actually a poem. Somehow, I thought it would make it easier.

*Dear Justin,*
*The way you make me feel is wrong my brotha*
*Because the reality is, you still belong to another*
*I understand you say your divorce is almost final*
*But how do I know, she won't be back*
*Because if I realize you are a good man,*
*She may once again realize the same thing*
*And want you to once again wear that wedding ring*
*Then what would I do, I'm in love with you*

*Being the family man that you are,*
*I know you would want to do what's right*
*But look at all the drama that it brings to your life*
*Is it worth the fussing and fighting,*
*That end with you sleeping in another room?*
*I want to say something,*
*But I don't know if it's safe to assume*
*Given the opportunity, I think you would stay for your kids*
*But ask yourself, is a loveless marriage*
*What a happy home is?*

*I'm sorry but I can't continue to fill that void*
*And I'm getting annoyed with this situation I put myself in*
*I can't even fault you,*
*Whenever I saw the sadness in your eyes*
*I took it upon myself to come to your rescue*

## K. Lowery Moore

*I wanted to help you through your pain*
*To help you regain your confidence as a black man,*
*My hero, always know that I am here for you*
*It bothers me to see all you allow yourself to go through*

*You shared with me the message she left calling you*
*All kinds of worthless bastards and no good niggas*
*So the way I figure, it's time for you to move on*
*Even if it's not with me,*
*Don't you see, the way you live is not healthy*
*Now I don't know what you've done,*
*Because it's always three sides*
*However, to me nothing will ever justify*
*Badmouthing a father to his child,*
*That is where I draw the line*
*But see, sometimes as women*
*We don't appreciate the good qualities that a man posses*
*Nevertheless, we are quick to stress*
*When we think he is less than his best*
*Instead of putting him down, we need to uplift him*
*It disturbs me to see what happens*
*To most of our good black men*
*I've seen women put men through some unnecessary hell*
*You're one of those men, baby I can tell*

*I see the good man that you are,*
*However, as women we all have a different definition*
*Trust me, deep down inside*
*I want to give you whatever you've been missing*
*But right now time is not on our side*
*Yes I love you, that's something I could never hide*
*Understand this is hurting me*

*When I'm Loving You*

*Probably more than it's hurting you
But please you have to let me go,
For now it's the best thing to do*

*Love Always,
Lynda*

A few days after I sent the poem to Justin, he called me on my cell phone to say that he would not bother me if I really loved Zion. I ensured him that he would always have a special place in my heart; however, I wanted to be with Zion. When our conversation ended, I still wasn't convinced that it was really over.

As I lay awake, waiting for Zion to come home, his house phone constantly rang. Normally I wouldn't answer his phone, although he said I could, but I noticed the same number on the caller ID several times. I wanted to make sure it wasn't some kind of emergency. After I answered the phone, I immediately wished I hadn't.

"Hello."

"Hello, may I speak to Zion?" A female voice asked.

"Zion is not here right now. Would you like to leave a message?"

"Yeah, would you tell him Jasmine called?"

*Jasmine*, I thought to myself. *Why does this voice sound familiar?* Then it dawned on me that it was Jasmine, bisexual Jasmine. *But, why would she be calling for Zion?* Lord knows I don't need anymore drama. I didn't respond, I just hung up the phone.

TO BE CONTINUED…

STAY TUNED FOR THE SEQUEL

# WHEN THE LOVING GETS TOO GOOD!

# Poems for Zion

# LET'S TALK POETRY
Copyright © 2007 by K. Lowery Moore

Let's talk poetry
Your place or mine
Burn incense, candles
Pour a couple of glasses of wine
Take our shoes off and relax
Massage each other's mind
I say one line then
You say the first thing that comes to your mind

Let's talk poetry
But first, let me straddle you
We're gonna still talk poetry
Because I am feeling you
A man that's not afraid to express
What's he's feeling I'm impressed
I wanna talk poetry
But first, let me undress

I just wanna give you a little inspiration
From the moment I first saw you,
I already had my motivation
I think this could be a serious work of art
The poetry we'd make together
But, before we start

Let's get you comfortable
Now isn't that better
You're all relaxed
And me, I'm getting wetter

We can take a break
If that's what you want to do
And I'll finish this poem
When I'm through sexing you

# SHOW AND TELL
Copyright ©2007 by K. Lowery Moore

I've been wondering what it would be like
to be close to you
Just the two of us face to face alone at my place
I've been fantasizing about what it would be like to
straddle you
Look into your eyes, kiss you softly
First on your lips, then on your neck,
then on your chest
And don't worry, for you, I won't neglect the rest
I also want you to explore my body
Every inch of me, slowly, show me how you do
Because I am so into you
So I've been wondering what it would be like for you
to be in me
Stroking deeply, damn freak me baby
on these silk sheets
Tasting me will be a treat
Don't you know how well chocolate goes with caramel?
So, I was wondering are you up for a game of
show and tell?
But, I can show you better than I can tell you
What I've been wanting to do to you!

## SOUL MATE
Copyright © 2007 by K. Lowery Moore

We communicate to each other without saying a word
Your thoughts speak to me when words are not heard
Though this may sound absurd to some,
Others know exactly what I mean
Whenever I'm near you, it's like I'm living in a dream
And, I don't want to wake up

I knew from the moment you sat down next to me; there was something between us
I've learned to trust my instincts because they are more than just….gut feelings
Even if we don't act on our feelings, it's no question the chemistry is there
But, not acting on our feelings the question is, would that be fair?

I've tried to play it off but we really can't hide it
Not to think about you, shit I've tried it
But, every time you walk by me or come near me
I swear my heart skips a few beats

And believe me, it's not easy dealing with this situation
Neither one of us needs this complication
Because you want to be faithful to her and I need to be faithful to him
But, if we aren't faithful to ourselves first, does anyone really win?

At night, whether or not I'm alone, I would rather you be there
I don't care how she is there for you; I don't care about what he does for me
Can't you see, your soul speaks to my soul and you can't get a deeper connection
This is more than simple affection

And, before you say it, it's not even about sex
You know that's not the mission, that's not what this is
It's much deeper than that and as a matter of fact
My feelings for you have reached a depth until now unknown
And although I'm grown
I'm standing here with a schoolgirl crush

And, I must tell you, it's not okay that you have her and I am with him
Understand I'm not pressuring you, but we also cannot pretend
It's very real, how we both feel
So let's just enjoy this like our first dance
But, think about it, nothing we do is simply by chance
We are where we are for a reason

And, in each season, God knows what He is doing
But, most of the time we fail to listen
So, ask yourself, in your relationship what are you missing?
The answer may very well be—your soul mate.

## YOUR WORDS
(Part 1 of 2)
Copyright © 2007 by K. Lowery Moore

Your words move me, soothe my massages my mind
Kisses the back of my neck and then slowly kisses down my spine
Caresses my hips, thigh and I don't want it to stop
So I turn myself over to let your words start again from the top
Your words kiss my lips, my breast and on down to my navel
I don't think you understand how your words got me
Ready, willing, and able
Your words have been like some kind of massage therapy
If your words got me like this,
I can't imagine what you would do to me

Your words move me, soothe me is this really poetry?
In and out my ear again, again and again,
Naw your words are making love to me
I know words are powerful but damn this is new to me
How is this happening?
Your words have satisfied me and provided me pleasure
This moment I will always treasure because never
Has anyone's words given me this sensational feeling
I wish could last forever.

## CAN I HAVE YOU TONIGHT?
(Part 2 of 2)
Copyright© 2007 by K. Lowery Moore

Can I have you tonight?
I know you can feel this chemistry between us
But neither one of us wants to make the first move
But I think one of us is gonna have to
Because you've teased me enough with your words
And I'm ready for you to please me in way unheard
Let's not talk about who we have or our pasts
Let's just make love and enjoy each other tonight

I need you to satisfy this yearning, I can't take it anymore
And I'm learning to go after what I'm longing for –You
This attraction is strong so what's wrong with sexing me tonight
You know what, I think that's a yes and I'll be willing to bet
Why? Because you haven't left yet
Look at you tryna act all hard, I mean you're hard I see
So quit playing with me

Well Imma make a move so you just relax
While I take off your shoes and those slacks
I can't even believe you're tryna fight this affection
With that kind of erection, and don't worry I have protection
All sizes, colors, flavors
That reminds me; let's see what's up wit the strawberry one later
I know you think I'm playing, but I'm very serious
And by the look on your face, I know you are curious
So let's just make love tonight
Alright?

I hope you have enjoyed my novel.
Share your thoughts with me by sending an email to
KLoweryMoore@aol.com

To schedule K. Lowery Moore for signings, book events, book club discussions, poetry readings or speaking engagements, please contact:

Lisa Smith, Author Relations
So Sophisticated Publications
LisaSmithPR@aol.com
(202) 903-5678

# QUICK ORDER FORM

I am enclosing $_____ (plus $4.25 USPS Priority shipping for the 1st book, $1.00 for each additional book). No cash or CODs please. Check, money order, certified check, MasterCard, Visa, and American Express are accepted forms of payment.

**SHIPPING INFORMATION:**

Name _____

Address _____

City _____ State _____ Zip Code _____

**METHOD OF PAYMENT:**

___ Check     ____ Money Order (Make payable to: So Sophisticated Publications)

___ American Express     ___ MasterCard     ____ Visa

Card Holder Name: _____

Account #: _____ Expiration Date: _____

Total amount to be charged: $_____

Authorized Signature: _____ Date: _____

Mail to:
So Sophisticated Publications
P.O. Box 23002
Washington, DC  20026-3002

Please allow 2 weeks for delivery. For express shipping or international costs, please call (202) 903-5678 for fees.

Printed in the United States
200317BV00002B/840/A